The Hedgehog's Dilemma

TOON TELLEGEN is one of the Netherlands' best-loved authors. A retired doctor, he initially found fame writing books for children, before beginning his hugely popular series of witty philosophical animal fables for adults. The series has sold more than a million copies in the Netherlands alone, and the books have also become international bestsellers, translated into 25 languages across the world. *The Cricket's Healing* is also forthcoming from Pushkin Press.

DAVID COLMER has won many prizes for his translations, including the IMPAC Dublin Literary Award and the *Independent* Foreign Fiction Prize (precursor to the International Booker Prize), both with novelist Gerbrand Bakker. He also translated Willem Frederik Hermans' *An Untouched House* and *A Guardian Angel Recalls* for Pushkin Press.

ANNEMARIE VAN HAERINGEN is an internationally renowned illustrator of picture books who lives in Amsterdam. Her books have been translated into many languages and won numerous awards.

The Hedgehog's Dilemma

TOON TELLEGEN

Translated from the Dutch by David Colmer

Illustrated by Annemarie Van Haeringen

PUSHKIN PRESS

Pushkin Press
Somerset House, Strand
London WC2R 1LA

Original title *Het verlangen van de egel*

First published in 2014 by Em. Querido's Uitgeverij, Amsterdam
First published by Pushkin Press in 2025

1 3 5 7 9 8 6 4 2

ISBN 13: 978-1-80533-171-1

Designed and typeset by Tetragon, London
Printed and bound in the United Kingdom by Clays Ltd, Elcograf S.p.A.

www.pushkinpress.com

1

One day in late autumn, the hedgehog was sitting by the window looking out.

He was alone. Nobody ever came to visit and if someone happened to be passing and thought, Oh, isn't this where Hedgehog lives? and rang the bell, the hedgehog would be sure to be asleep or else he'd hesitate for so long they'd have already walked on again before he'd made it to the door.

He pressed his nose against the glass, screwed up his eyes and thought of the animals he knew, who were always constantly visiting each other, sometimes for no reason at all, never waiting for a birthday or something else to celebrate. What if I invited them here for once… he thought.

He had never invited anyone anywhere.

He opened his eyes again, scratched between the prickles on the back of his head, thought for a little longer and then wrote a letter:

Dear animals,

I hereby invite all of you to come and visit me.

Chewing his pen, he gave the back of his head another scratch, then wrote at the bottom.

But if nobody comes, that's okay too.

He frowned.

If they read this letter, he thought, won't they think, The hedgehog doesn't really want any visitors…? Or maybe, Quick, let's go and visit right away while he still wants us to… the hedgehog's always changing his mind…?

I can't decide, he thought.

He put the letter in a drawer of his cupboard and shook his head. I won't send it, he thought. Not yet.

2

Not yet. The hedgehog sat down by the window again and thought about those two words. Not and Yet.

It was like they were dancing inside his head. Not was turning circles with measured steps. Yet was looking around uncertainly.

The hedgehog closed his eyes. Now I can see them better, he thought. Not grabbed hold of Yet and Yet cuddled up to Not. They were dancing and only had eyes for each other.

But suddenly the door opened and another word came in. That's Just, thought the hedgehog. He could tell from its coat, which was almost too small.

Just went over to Not and Yet, squeezed in between them and joined the dance. The hedgehog sighed.

After a while Just slipped away and Anytime came stomping in. It was wearing a hat and a thickly quilted winter coat, and it too pushed in between Not and Yet.

The hedgehog felt his heart pounding. It was like the words were dancing towards him, straight through his thoughts, and expecting something from him. As if he was supposed to do something with them. He didn't know what.

The three words leapt up onto the table and kept dancing, faster and faster and more and more furiously. The hedgehog could hardly bear to watch and was about to close his mind's eye and open his real ones. But suddenly Anytime disappeared.

Not and Yet climbed down from the table and stood there indecisively, looking at each other. More dancing? Not raised its eyebrows. It was willing, but Yet shook its head.

The hedgehog heard a racket outside. The door opened again and Just came back in with Once. They were in high spirits. Skipping and cooing. They both had funny red feathers in their hair.

Just and Once grabbed Not and Yet and, in the same instant, calmed down and began a stately four-person dance.

It had grown dark in the hedgehog's room.

Yet Not Just Once, he thought, and Yet danced away for a moment, leaving Not Just Once. And Not swirled off after Yet. Just Once. Just Once.

And suddenly it was glorious the way they were dancing together, and the hedgehog thought, Dance on like that forever. Because beyond those words everything was black.

3

Games, thought the hedgehog, reopening his eyes. Get a grip. This is about visitors and that's no game.

He lay down on his bed and thought about the letter in the cupboard drawer.

Maybe they'll write back that they can't come. All of them. They'll have their reasons.

The hedgehog could already see dozens of letters blowing in under the door. He picked them up and read them one after the other:

'If I come to visit, I want a three-storey honey cake covered with icing and with a whipped-cream fountain on top under a fondant sky, but I don't think I can make it.'

'I came to visit just the other day, but you didn't open up. I looked in

through the window just in time to see you crawling under your bed.'

'Thanks for the invite! Come and visit! You! How lovely! I was over the moon when I read your letter! Hedgehog, visit Hedgehog… But I can't.'

'I think I won't be able to come. I just don't know the reason yet.'

'I'll be there in spirit.'

'Best wishes in lieu of a visit.'

The hedgehog sighed. Of course nobody will come.

He piled the letters up on the floor next to the bed and turned onto his back, feeling relieved and sad at the same time. I am made to be lonely, he thought, just like I'm made to be prickly. If I had wings instead of prickles I wouldn't be this lonely. I'd fly wherever I wanted to go and never be wistful about anything again.

He wanted to get some sleep but couldn't. Maybe everyone will come after all, he thought.

He shivered, got up and made himself some tea. Two cups.

4

After drinking the tea, the hedgehog got the letter out of the drawer and read through it.

Maybe they'll come right away, he thought. All at once. First thing tomorrow morning.

He felt a chill pass through him and put down the letter. He could already hear the animals approaching. The forest seemed to be quivering with excitement.

They were milling around in front of the door, shouting, 'Hedgehog! We're here! Your visitors! Thanks for the invitation! Everyone's made it! Nobody's missing!'

They pushed the door open and stormed in. Most of them were walking, flying or crawling, but the pike and the carp, and a little later the whale and the shark, swam in on big waves they'd brought with them for the occasion.

'What fun, Hedgehog!' they all cried. 'Do you have tea? And cake?'

There were too many animals to make tea for. And

there was only one small, slightly stale cake. The hedgehog shrugged helplessly.

'It doesn't matter,' they cried, 'we'll just dance.'

They wrapped their arms around each other's shoulders and danced around the table, singing, 'We're Hedgehog's… we're Hedgehog's… we're Hedgehog's visitors. Everyone has made it and we don't need to eat.'

'But aren't you scared of me?' the hedgehog asked, sticking his prickles up as straight as he could.

'Not at all,' they cried. 'We're way too happy to be scared.'

In no time the floor caved in under their dancing, making a hole for the mole and the worm to creep up through, calling out that they were coming to visit too. They had brought some mud pies, which stayed good for years, according to them, but could also be eaten straight away if you preferred.

'Who'd expected something like this?' they all asked.

Not me, thought the hedgehog. He slipped outside and crawled into the bushes behind the house.

Soon after, the animals stopped dancing, having noticed that the hedgehog was gone.

'Hedgehog, Hedgehog!' they cried.

Their calls could be heard far beyond the forest and soon the camel and the termite came running in from the desert. They didn't want to be left out.

'Hedgehog, Hedgehog, Hedgehog...' they kept shouting together.

But the hedgehog crept deeper and deeper into the bushes.

He shook his head, changed 'all of you' to 'one of you', put 'at most' in front of that and read the letter once again.

5

No, he thought, if I do that, they could still all come at once.

He chewed his pen and pondered. If I don't send it, nobody will come. That's for sure. They won't turn up uninvited.

Deep furrows appeared on his forehead. They're scared of me, he thought. They just don't dare to admit it. They're in awe of my prickles. When they get together, they tell each other that no matter what happens, they'll never come to visit me.

'I'll visit anyone. But not the hedgehog.'

'Me neither.'

'It's those prickles…'

'Yes, those terrible prickles…'

'You know what they're for?'

'No.'

'To scare us off.'

'Really?'

'Yes.'

The hedgehog put the letter back.

They're right, he thought. I scare them off. He shuddered and for a moment his prickles swayed from side to side.

It was like there was someone running around inside his body and shaking it here and there, trying to get out. But I'm not scary at all! he thought.

The hedgehog felt like opening his door and rushing outside to stand on his toes and shout, 'Animals! It's me! Hedgehog! I'm really nice! I'm not scary!'

Then their eyes would be opened and they'd all call back, 'Hedgehog! You're right! You don't scare anyone! You couldn't scare us if you tried! You're the kindest animal we know. If you invite us, we'll all come to visit. Those prickles of yours are really no big deal…'

The hedgehog felt even deeper furrows forming between the prickles on his forehead and wrote a footnote at the bottom of the letter:

My prickles are really no big deal

He chewed his pen, thought for a long time and put the letter back in the drawer.

My prickles are a big deal, he thought. My prickles are a very big deal.

He nodded. A bigger deal than me.

6

Maybe animals are visiting each other everywhere right this moment, he thought a little later. Maybe they're asking each other, 'By the way, are you perhaps by any chance going to visit the hedgehog sometime soon?'

'No – you?'

'No, me neither. I haven't been invited.'

'Me neither.'

'It's a shame, isn't it?'

'Yes, a great shame.'

'If he invited me, I'd go.'

'Me too.'

'It's up to him.'

'Yes. If he doesn't invite us, we won't invite him either.'

'No, we won't.'

They shrug. Now. Right this moment. Everywhere in the forest. At sea. In the desert. Behind the clouds. Everyone visiting everyone else. Except me. They're all dancing with each other and talking about me and shrugging.

He felt himself growing very sad and went outside to listen if he could hear the hubbub of any parties anywhere.

But it was quiet in the forest. Very far away he heard the elephant falling out of a tree and a little closer he heard the frog trying to croak out a few notes she couldn't quite reach.

Then he thought, Maybe all that visiting has come to an end; maybe it's no longer allowed.

He imagined enormous signs with:

AS OF NOW,
VISITING STRICTLY PROHIBITED

and

AS OF NOW,
RECEIVING VISITORS STRICTLY PROHIBITED

written on them.

Maybe nobody will go to visit anybody else ever again and they'll only write each other letters, but less and less often and shorter and shorter too:

Hi Hedgehog,
That's all.

and:

Dear Fly,

I

and nothing else.

Then he wouldn't need to invite anyone after all.

He pricked up his ears. He thought he could hear distant, very sad sighs coming from all directions, because there was nothing the animals liked more than visiting each other and writing letters.

But rules are rules.

What shall I do? he thought. He got the letter out of the drawer, read it twice, looked down at his toes, thought about it and put it back again.

I don't know, he thought.

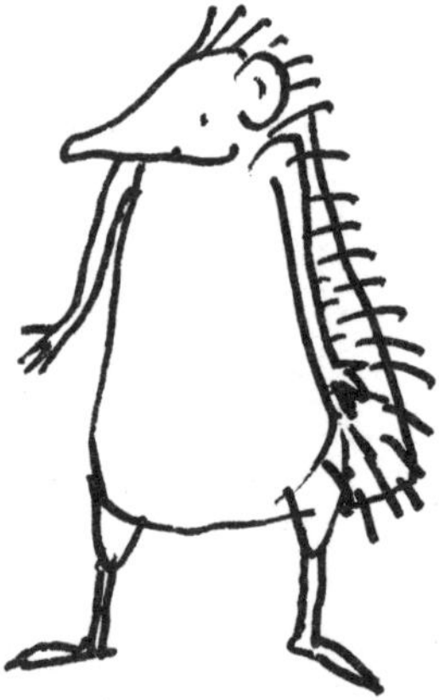

7

The hedgehog stood in front of his cupboard, thought about the letter and shook his head. But immediately afterwards he changed his mind, nodded, shook his head again and nodded once more.

Sometimes he did that a hundred times a day. There's nothing my mind likes more than changing, he thought. And me? There's nothing I can do about it. I'm at its mercy.

He gave a little cough, straightened his back and thought about animals he knew well who would be sure to come to visit if he invited them.

The longhorn beetle, for instance… He scratched the back of his head.

No, he thought, I'm wrong, he definitely wouldn't come. My invitation would annoy him. Yet another animal who wants something from him. He'd write a letter in reply:

Dear Hedgehog,

I won't come to visit you.

You're bound to want me to do something for you.

You'll want skin without prickles.

Or two horns on your head. (Who wouldn't want two horns on their head?)

Or to never rustle again.

Or to be able to sing.

Or all that at once.

Why don't you just stay like you are?

Lonely, unsure about everything, a little sad, but also slightly happy?

Why don't you just make up animals that come to visit – talk to them, dance with them, have them tell you how nice you are, much nicer than they thought?

LONGHORN

That's what he'd write, thought the hedgehog.

He nodded again and wrote a letter back to the longhorn:

Dear Longhorn,

Thank you very much for your letter.

You're right, I want all of that.

I'll make up visitors and stay just the way I am.

HEDGEHOG

He wrote this letter no less than ten times, and every time he left something out, until there was nothing left of it at all.

It doesn't matter, he thought. The longhorn beetle won't come anyway. He's the only one who definitely won't.

But he wanted the longhorn beetle to be the only one who did come. Then he – the hedgehog – wouldn't ask him anything and they'd drink a cup of tea without talking, just nodding at each other, and after they'd finished, the longhorn beetle would go back home again.

He went over to his window and looked out. In his imagination, animals were approaching from all directions. They called out, 'Hedgehog! Hedgehog! We're coming to visit! Thanks for inviting us!'

He felt like shouting, 'I'm not home!' But instead he said, 'Fine.'

8

The snail and the tortoise, he thought, sitting down at his table. If I invite them, they'll start getting ready to come over right away.

He pictured them.

'Let's go,' said the tortoise. She'd polished her shell so well it was shining in the sun and reflecting the treetops.

But the snail shook his head. 'It's not a good time for me right now,' he said.

'Tomorrow?'

'No, not tomorrow either.'

'When is?'

The snail thought for a moment. The two tentacles on his head wobbled softly to and fro. 'Never,' he said. 'It will never be a good time.' When he stopped to think about it, he realised that it was never a good time for anything.

The tortoise looked at the ground and pulled her head back into her shell.

'It's a good time for you, of course,' the snail cried. 'It's always a good time for everything for you. Admit it!'

The tortoise disappeared completely into her shell.

'Of course!' the snail shouted. 'Back into your shell! Leave me to it again. Your friend.'

He felt like stamping his foot.

Then he took a step forward. 'I'm on my way,' he said. 'Don't worry.'

The tortoise came back out of her shell and took a step too.

'But only because you insist. Do you know who you are really?' the snail said.

'No.'

'Not the tortoise.'

'No?'

'No. The bully. Look, who's that going past? That's the bully. Oh, she is such a bully! You can say that again. Don't get me started… As if that visit can't wait! And tomorrow we'll go and visit the polar bear, I suppose. And the day after, someone on the moon. Feel free. One invitation after the other. No, don't worry about the suffering you're causing others. Rushing them along. Wearing them out. Exhausting them. That's what you do! You didn't know that, did you? No, you didn't know. You only think of one thing. Yourself. That's right. Do you know what else you are?'

'No,' the tortoise said.

'Selfish. Selfish through and through.'

The snail had taken another step while talking and now he stopped.

He was worn out. The distance to the hedgehog's house was beyond his powers of imagination. He felt like not doing anything. Just grumbling and nothing else.

The tortoise stopped now too and thought of the winter, when she could finally have a very long, very deep sleep inside her shell.

9

The hedgehog got up, paced the room for a while and then lay down on his bed.

He decided to stay put for a while. If I get up, I'll just start thinking again, he thought. And if I think, I'll start doubting again. That's what always happens. He sighed. Maybe I have more doubts than prickles. It's a good thing doubts are invisible. Although… Maybe they are visible. Maybe everyone can see them but me. The hedgehog… do you mean the animal with all those doubts? Yes, that's him. He's got so many! A thousand at least. Look at them shine! He's like the sun!

He closed his eyes. I always doubt things, he thought, and sometimes I'm sad. But I'm never at my wit's end. That's impossible.

The hedgehog knew that if he was in danger of getting close to his wit's end, an inner voice would say, 'Whoa!' Otherwise he would crash into something he should never crash into, no matter what.

Then he thought of the toad, who definitely didn't have an inner voice that said 'Whoa!' when he was getting angry about something.

It was early in the morning. Someone knocked on the door.

'Yes,' he said.

The toad came in.

'Hello, Hedgehog,' he said.

'Hello, Toad,' said the hedgehog.

'I've come to visit.'

'Okay.'

The toad looked around.

They drank some tea and sat across from each other for a long time without saying anything. When the tea's finished, he might go away again, thought the hedgehog. Then I'll have had my unexpected visitor and after that nobody else will need to come here ever again.

But the toad cleared his throat and said, 'I'd like to get angry, Hedgehog.'

'Why?' asked the hedgehog.

'That's what I always want when I go to visit someone. Anger is so wonderful... Cake's nothing by comparison.'

The hedgehog didn't say anything. He never got angry.

'I want to get furious,' the toad continued. 'So angry I swell up and explode with rage.' He looked at the hedgehog. 'You have to make me angry.'

'I don't think I can,' said the hedgehog.

'Of course you can!' the toad shouted, jumping up onto his feet. 'I'm visiting you, aren't I? Am I your guest or not? I want to get angry *now*!'

'But how—'

'Tell me what you think of me! Horrible! Stupid! Ugly! If only I hadn't come to visit! Why do I even exist? Your whole winter ruined! By me!'

He swung his fists around.

'But I don't think any of that,' the hedgehog said.

'You do think it!' the toad screamed. 'You have to!' He swelled up enormously and turned dark green. Slowly he began to fill the hedgehog's entire room. 'Now!' he screeched. 'You have to think it now!'

'I think you're horrible…' the hedgehog whispered, looking down at the floor.

'What?' bellowed the toad. 'What's that you're saying? You think I'm horrible…?'

Then he couldn't swell up any more or turn any darker and he exploded with a furious but blissful look in his eyes.

The hedgehog turned onto his side. I was planning on lying here a little longer and not thinking about things… he thought. That didn't work out.

10

I'll have to do up my house if I want visitors, he thought.

He was in bed. He'd forgotten the toad and was imagining furnishing a special room for visitors, in case they didn't come separately but all at once because they all thought they were the only one who'd been invited. A reception room. Everyone could walk around it and sit down in it. He'd put a pond in one corner for the animals who like to visit underwater, like the pike and the carp and the stickleback.

At the back of the reception room, he'd make a room for himself, somewhere off limits to visitors. He'd hang a little sign on the door, saying:

THIS ROOM IS ONLY FOR ME.
NO ENTRY. NO KNOCKING.
THE HEDGEHOG

A place he could withdraw to.

He would drill a little hole in the wall so he could look through it at his visitors.

Maybe they'd all be standing in the reception room and asking each other, 'Where is the hedgehog anyway? We're visiting him, aren't we? Doesn't he live here?'

'Don't ask me.'

Then he'd call out, 'I'll be there in a second!' but then he'd stay where he was. And if they knocked, he'd call, 'Just a minute!'

At the end of the day his visitors would go away, maybe without having seen him, and he'd whirl around the big reception room by himself.

That was actually what he wanted most of all, to whirl around by himself. Visitors were incidental. An intermezzo, the ant had once told him. Maybe he needed to write that in his letter too:

You are an intermezzo in my existence.

But maybe they didn't know what an intermezzo was and thought it was a kind of hullaballoo, and then they'd bring horns with them and enormous drums and start yelling and screaming before they'd even come close to his house…

He decided not to add it to his letter and on second thoughts he decided not to do up his house either.

They have to take me as I am, he thought, prickles and all.

11

The hedgehog pulled up the blanket and tried to go to sleep but couldn't.

Suddenly the rhino appeared in his thoughts. He was already at the door and knocking. The rhino… the hedgehog thought and let out a deep sigh.

Then he screwed up his courage. He's come to visit, he thought. I invited him.

'Come in,' he said.

'Hello, Hedgehog,' the rhino said, and stepped in through the door.

'Hello, Rhino,' the hedgehog said. He wanted to tell him that he thought it was really nice that he'd come to visit and he wanted to point out where he could sit and tell him that it would only take a moment and he'd have some tea ready and that he knew the rhino would undoubtedly leave again after the tea, because he was sure to have other things to do that day, as he undoubtedly had lots to do every day of the week. But the rhino came round the table, seized the hedgehog and wrapped his arms around him.

'What a surprise, Hedgehog,' he said, 'that invitation! I've been wanting to come to visit you for a very long time, but I always thought you didn't want me to… because I always knock everyone over and always push in front of everyone else and stand on their toes… but it's really not that bad, you know… Shall we dance?'

And without waiting for an answer, because he never did, he picked the hedgehog up and spun him around. The hedgehog didn't say anything and let himself be dragged along, through the room and outside too, and around the house, and the rhino threw him up into the air a few times, and he was just able to grab hold of the rhino's horn. The rhino was singing while he danced, and they both kept shouting 'Ouch!' because the hedgehog was jabbing the rhino's stomach with his prickles and the rhino was stepping on the hedgehog's toes.

Finally they stumbled over each other's legs, fell over and lay stretched out on the ground.

'That was so lovely…' the rhino mumbled. 'I love dancing so much!' He pulled a few prickles out of his stomach as he struggled back up onto his feet.

The hedgehog stayed where he was. The few prickles he had left were all bent or bruised. He was finding it a rather difficult visit. I should have worn heavy boots, he thought. I should have said I can't dance. I should have made tea right away. I should have done so many things.

'So,' the rhino said. 'I'm off again.'

'Okay,' the hedgehog whispered.

'If you'd like another visit, just let me know. We can dance some more. I know some other steps too, very special ones. Bye, Hedgehog.'

12

I might as well get up, thought the hedgehog, swinging his legs over the side of the bed.

While he was still sitting there, the bear appeared in his thoughts for no apparent reason, stepping in through the door unexpectedly.

'That invitation, Hedgehog, that's what I'm here for,' he said, quickly looking around.

'Hello, Bear,' the hedgehog said.

'I suppose you're going to make some tea for me,' the bear said, 'and that's fine too, but do you have anything to go with it?'

'Yes,' the hedgehog said.

'What?'

'I'll just have to look in the cupboard. You've come so unexpectedly...'

'Let me look,' the bear said.

He opened the cupboard and saw a jar of linden honey on the top shelf.

'Shall I eat this first, while you put on the kettle?' he asked, opening the jar and sticking his tongue into it.

'Fine,' the hedgehog said and put the kettle on.

'And otherwise?' the bear asked, when he'd finished the honey and the tea still wasn't ready.

'Wait a second…' the hedgehog said.

'Why?' the bear asked. 'Don't you know what else you've got? Shall I help look for something?'

He looked on all of the shelves in the cupboard, and then under the cupboard, but couldn't find anything.

When the hedgehog put two cups of tea on the table a moment later, the bear was lying half under the bed, groping around.

'Nothing here,' he said.

'No,' said the hedgehog, who never kept anything there at all.

The bear re-emerged from under the bed. He looked in the corners of the room and knocked on the walls to see if there were any secret stashes anywhere.

'Nothing,' he said at last.

'No,' the hedgehog said. 'I don't have anything else at home. I've…' He didn't finish because the bear had climbed onto the table and was looking in the lightshade, where he thought there was sure to be another jar of honey or else a honey cake or something special for unexpected visitors, something extremely delicious that he'd never even tasted. But there wasn't anything there either.

'Forget it,' he said, taking a step away from the table. He shrugged and looked around the room one last time. 'I'll go and visit someone else,' he mumbled, left the room and ran off into the forest.

13

I have to bake a cake, no matter what, thought the hedgehog. A cake for everyone who comes to visit.

He nodded and decided to bake the cake first and only then send the letter with the invitation.

He tried to think of something all the animals would like. I have to take everyone into account, he thought.

That meant it had to be a honey cake, but also a cream cake, a mud cake, an oak-bark cake, a beach-grass cake, a cuttlebone cake, a dead-nettle cake, a hollyhock cake, a bird's-foot-trefoil cake, a waterlily cake, a moss cake, a…

He kept thinking of something else a particular animal was especially keen on.

The cake got bigger and bigger, so to make room, the hedgehog took his table, his chair, his cupboard and his bed outside, around the back of his house.

But it also had to be a silt cake, a lagoon-sludge cake, a fleawort cake, a willow-root cake, a powdery-snow cake…

The cake filled the whole room, broke through the ceiling and, immediately after that, through the roof, as well as bulging out through the window and pushing open the door. And it hasn't even started to rise yet, thought the hedgehog.

He stood at the base of the cake and looked up.

When the cake stretched up higher than the trees next to his house and into the clouds, he thought of someone coming to visit, seeing the cake, and asking, 'What's that?'

'A cake,' said the hedgehog.

'A cake?' the visitor cried. 'I don't want any cake! I want all kinds of things, but no cake!' And they turned and ran off in a fury, shouting, 'Call that a visit…' over their shoulder.

And the next visitor said, 'I love cake. There's nothing I like more. But not with mud in it!' And the visitor after that listed a hundred kinds of cake they loved, but lagoon-sludge cake wasn't one of them.

All day long, animals came to visit, saw the cake, pointed something out, asked what it was, flinched and left. And they told everyone they met, 'Are you going to visit the hedgehog?'

'Yes.'

'Don't go! Don't go! He's baked a hideous cake.'

'Really?'

'Yes. The most hideous cake you've ever seen.'

And then the other animals turned back too.

Maybe I should just make a cake I like myself. Then if somebody doesn't like it or thinks it's too small, I'll just eat it.

He took a deep breath and thought, I'll see. He nodded. First I have to get up.

14

I won't invite anyone, he thought after he'd got up. That's much more sensible.

He looked at his feet.

But will that mean I'll keep getting lonelier? Until I'm a lot lonelier than I am now?

He imagined toppling off a cliff and falling down, down, with no bottom in sight. He was spinning around, his prickles all standing on end.

Is that what Loneliness wants from me?

He didn't understand Loneliness's intentions. What do you want from me? he sometimes whispered in the dark when he felt terribly lonely. He'd hear noises too; sometimes he'd even hear something that sounded like someone clearing their throat. But no answer came.

'Am I not allowed to know?' he whispered.

Again those noises and the clearing of a throat.

Loneliness's throat, he thought.

He stood next to his bed and tried to imagine Loneliness suddenly disappearing and everyone rushing in. Or better yet, *one* somebody opening the door and coming in and Loneliness slipping out past them.

It would be an extraordinarily nice and friendly somebody, thought Hedgehog. Somebody who always brings beechnut honey with them when they come to visit.

They'd drink some tea. They'd talk about all kinds of things. They would decide to go on a trip together and a little later they'd change their minds and decide not to. They'd look out and see that night was falling. They would stay quiet for a very long time and nod now and then and clear their throats.

And then Loneliness would come back again.

'What just came in?' the visitor would ask.

'Loneliness,' the hedgehog would say.

'Does it live here?'

'Well, I wouldn't call it living. It's here. It comes and goes.'

'Oh.'

And even if they hadn't finished their tea yet and still had something very important to say to each other, they would both feel very lonely.

'What's this feeling I suddenly have?' the visitor would ask.

'*My* feeling,' the hedgehog would whisper.

It had grown dark. The visitor would leave without another word. Loneliness would stay.

15

The hedgehog could feel the deep wrinkles on his forehead.

I'm not really lonely, am I? he thought. I've always got myself. I talk to myself, don't I? I can see myself. I'm always here, aren't I?

He got up, walked over to the mirror and looked at himself while rocking back and forth on his toes.

'Hello, self,' he said quietly. 'I see you. You can't hide from me. You'll never manage that. But you've got secrets from me. Don't deny it. I can see it in your face. That mouth of yours… Spit it out! What do you know about me?'

He shook his head. If you're really alone, you can't do that, he thought. There's nobody to keep secrets from.

He stared hard at himself. Maybe I should give myself a slap, he thought. Box my ears so I fall over shouting, 'You had that coming! Yes, you! Why? Because I'm not allowed to know what you're thinking!' If I didn't have prickles, I'd do it. A hard slap over the ears.

He sighed. Myself… he thought scornfully. What if that whole self didn't even exist… could that be possible? If I looked in the mirror and didn't see anyone… Then I'd really be alone!

He shuddered, sat down on the bed and pulled the blanket over his feet, which were ice-cold. Myself… he thought. Who is that, anyway? The myself. He is tired. He is hungry. He wants to sleep. He looks out of the window. He writes a letter and invites everyone to come and visit.

He slapped his forehead. He lives here.

Inside here! Myself. Yes, you! Ouch!

Then he bent forward and carefully pulled a prickle out of his hand.

16

He went back to the window and looked out. The sky was dark and one of the last leaves left on the oak tree broke loose and came floating down.

He imagined a visitor arriving the next day, just one.

The elephant.

'Hello, Hedgehog,' he said.

'Hello, Elephant,' said the hedgehog.

'I've come to visit.'

'Okay.'

The elephant sat down and the hedgehog made some tea.

'What shall we talk about?' the elephant asked.

The hedgehog knew that if you had visitors, you had to talk about something, but he didn't know what.

'I don't know,' he said.

They both sipped their tea and tried to think of something. But they couldn't.

The elephant looked around. There was a chair at the window.

'Hedgehog…' the elephant asked.

'Yes,' said the hedgehog.

'Is it all right if I put that chair on the table?'

'Yes,' said the hedgehog, who thought that you always had to accept everything your visitors suggested.

The elephant put the chair on the table.

'And is it all right if I climb onto the table and then up on the chair?' he asked.

'Yes.'

The elephant climbed up onto the table and then on the chair.

'And if I now stand on the back of the chair?'

'Yes.'

'On one leg?'

'Yes, even on one leg.'

The elephant stood on the back of the chair on one leg.

'And if I do a pirouette? Is that all right too? I can do it. Look'

But before the hedgehog could say that it was all right by him, even if he didn't really think it was all right, the elephant had done half a pirouette and had fallen, chair and all, on the table and then right through the table onto the floor.

'Ow,' he said. He rubbed the back of his head and pushed the pieces of broken table and chair to one side. He gave the hedgehog a crestfallen look.

No, thought the hedgehog, I hope the elephant doesn't come to visit tomorrow. And just to be on the safe side, he crawled under his bed.

17

But maybe someone will come to visit when I'm here under my bed, he thought after he'd been there for a while. What do I do then? Should I call out, 'I'm under the bed. Just a moment!' or should I pretend I'm not here?

He imagined the giraffe coming in. First her horns, then her neck and then the rest of her.

She looked around. The hedgehog's not home, she thought. Just to be on the safe side, she stuck her head under the cupboard, under the table and under the bed.

'There you are!' she cried. 'What fun! Under the bed! I thought you'd have a surprise for me! On the way here I said to myself, "Yes, the hedgehog, you never know where you are with him..." Have you been lying there on the floor for long? I'm going to start doing it too, getting under the bed when visitors come, but then with a sign on the door: A WARM WELCOME. VISIT ME UNDER THE BED, otherwise they'll keep going and I'll be lying there for no reason, and

I could also have a party under my bed – yes, that's what I'll do! I'll invite everyone. I've got a big bed. Everyone can fit under it: the elephant, the bear, the cricket, the rhino, the swan, everyone, and if they think it's too stuffy under there, I'll shout, "That's the whole idea! It's a stuffy party!" And if they want something to eat or drink and it's so full that nobody under the bed can get out, I'll shout, "It's a party without the fuss! That's what it's called!" They'll talk about it for years. Remember? What? The party without the fuss, under Giraffe's bed… Of course I remember. I always forget parties, but not that one…'

She talked nonstop and found it very cosy with her head under the bed.

The hedgehog didn't say anything and lay there squashed between the wall and the giraffe's head.

The giraffe started to tell him about her horns, which she was now forced to hold flat against her head.

'It's very cramped for them here, Hedgehog,' she said. 'I feel them grumbling. But I take that in my stride. You hear that? Grumble away.'

She said that it was actually very good for them. Adversity. Now and then. They always led such a regal existence up there on her head. So comfy. Never doing anything and still getting a bird's eye view of everything.

'I wish I was a horn, Hedgehog. And that they were me

and I was on their heads. They wouldn't know what hit them. Yes, you. I'm talking about you. But not an ill word about them,' she went on, while the horns on her head waved to and fro excitedly. She squinted at the hedgehog. 'Would you like to be a horn sometime too? And one of the horns would be you and you'd be on her back? Or would you prefer to be both at once?'

'I don't know,' the hedgehog said, wondering how long the visit was going to last.

Now the giraffe wanted to talk about the time she visited the whale. She'd gone there by boat. The whale was surprised to see her and entertained her under her fountain. 'Lovely, Hedgehog. Just like rain.' They'd talked for hours about the differences between whalebone and horn, and also the similarities, and the shark had dropped by too, and the flying fish…

'You can go again now,' said the hedgehog, who didn't feel any need to find out about the rest of the giraffe's visit with the whale.

'Thank you so much,' the giraffe said. She crawled back out from under the bed. 'What a visit! Just what I needed, Hedgehog, do you know that? Will you come and visit me too sometime? Under my bed?'

The hedgehog made a noise that could mean Yes or No and the giraffe went out of the door.

The hedgehog heard her outside, excitedly telling animals who happened to be passing by that she'd just visited the hedgehog. Under his bed!

'Under his bed?' they asked.

'Yes, under his bed. Lovely. He entertains everyone there.'

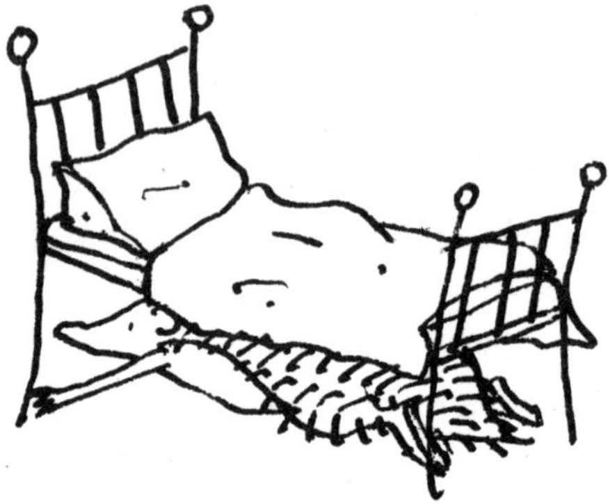

18

Or the ostrich, maybe the ostrich would come to visit, the hedgehog thought in the darkness under his bed.

He'd never met the ostrich, but the ant had told him that you always had to make sure to have something the ostrich could stick her head in.

'Like what?' the hedgehog had asked. The ant had shrugged and said, 'You'll see.'

You'll see… The hedgehog thought about those words. What would he see? What could it be? The sky? Maybe the ostrich wanted to stick her head in the sky. Or in a wall.

The ostrich came in. 'Hello, Hedgehog.'

'Hello, Ostrich. Would you like a cup of tea?'

'Yes, please, but first I'd like to stick my head in something.'

'Yes, of course. What do you like to stick it in the most?'

The ostrich looked around. Now I'll see, thought the hedgehog.

The ostrich saw the cupboard, walked around it once, pulled open a drawer and stuck her head in it. But she soon pulled it back out again.

'No…' she mumbled.

She got down on her knees and in turn stuck her head under the bed, behind the mirror and out of the window. But each time she pulled it back and shook it.

She thought all those places were musty or too cold.

The hedgehog made some tea.

'I don't know,' the ostrich said. 'There's not much choice.' She even stuck her head in the lampshade and then tried to wriggle it in between the hedgehog's prickles.

'Ow,' she said.

'That won't work,' the hedgehog said.

'No.'

The ostrich sat down on a chair and stared sadly at the feathers on her chest. She'd already stuck her head in between them so often; she hadn't come here for that.

The hedgehog put a cup of tea down in front of her.

'I'm sorry,' the ostrich said, 'I'd expected more from this visit.'

'Yes,' the hedgehog said. 'I have cake.'

But the ostrich went out of the door without drinking the tea, without seeing what kind of cake the hedgehog had made, and without another word.

The hedgehog looked through the window and saw her running off until, a little further along, with a raucous cry, she stuck her head in the ground at the base of the linden tree. Clods of earth flew up into the air.

19

Still lying under his bed, the hedgehog thought of the snail and the tortoise again.

It was already late in the morning. The tortoise was in front and turned to look at the snail, who was trailing behind her. 'We do need to hurry a little…' she said carefully.

'Hurry! You and your hurry…' the snail exclaimed, immediately stopping and even taking a small step back. 'Don't you know how terribly hurtful I find that word?'

The tortoise didn't reply. She didn't like the word either and she was sorry she'd used it.

'No, you don't know!' the snail yelled. 'All you know is hurry, faster, right this minute, now, immediately, at once, quick, quick…' It was like he was spitting the words out.

His tentacles had turned bright red and he crept back into his shell.

'Shall I write to him that we *are* coming, but we'll be a little late?' the tortoise asked.

'Write what you like!' shouted the snail, who was trying to calm down.

The tortoise pulled a piece of paper out from under her shell and wrote to the hedgehog that he mustn't be offended, but they would arrive a little late. She hoped the hedgehog would understand. They were both rather slow. They couldn't change that and they didn't want to. They detested speed.

She chewed on her pen for a moment. She loved the word 'detest'. Speed, haste and impatience were all detestable.

The snail came back out of his shell and said, 'Write that we're not coming at all.' He loved the words 'not at all'. He wished he wasn't called the snail, but the notatall. That's where the notatall lives... he doesn't walk, doesn't think, doesn't talk at all... He'd live up to his name.

But the tortoise didn't write that.

'He invited us. We have to go,' she said.

'Have to, have to... You and your have to the whole day long...'

'It's only polite.'

'Polite! Even worse!' The snail started ranting and roaring and accidentally bashed his head right through the roof of his shell.

'Look...' he cried. 'Guess whose fault that is!'

The tortoise helped him fix his shell. Then they continued on their way in silence.

'It will be nice,' the tortoise said after a while.

The snail didn't reply and, muttering to himself, slid forward millimetre by millimetre towards the closest blade of grass, where he planned to stop and catch his breath.

I wonder if they'll show up if I invite them, thought the hedgehog. Maybe next year, getting on for summer. And otherwise the year after that.

20

Or would all kinds of animals I've never even heard of come? he then thought in the dark under his bed. The desert worm, the sea mouse, the flying crab, the nightsnake…

They were already jostling in and looking around with surprise.

They didn't know what they were doing there and most of them didn't even know they existed.

The animals that were wearing coats hung them on the hedgehog's prickles, so in no time he had a good hundred exotic coats hanging on him and couldn't move any more.

'Would you care for something to drink? Tea perhaps?' he asked.

Caring for something to drink? They'd never cared for their drinks. And they'd never heard of tea.

A few of the unlikeliest animals ate the table and chairs. They thought the hedgehog had put them out for them.

They did like them, they said, but preferred sweet tables and fresh chairs.

Others asked where the visit was. They thought that a visit was something you could hold in your hands, maybe like a coat or a hat the hedgehog wanted to give them for winter. They'd all love a warm visit.

Or maybe it was something they could sit on.

New animals kept arriving. The sand drone, the airlion, the striped mud beetle, the ginger sloth…

They ate his curtains, his mirror and his bed, and nibbled on his prickles.

When there was nothing left of his house and his furniture, and most of his prickles were gone, they all pulled on the wrong coat, tumbled over each other and grabbed hold of the hedgehog's few remaining prickles, flipping him onto his back, then asked if anything special was about to happen, something astonishing, perhaps… they loved astonishment… and they still didn't know where the visit they'd been invited for was. It couldn't be a hat, anyway. Otherwise they'd have seen it.

Finally they all disappeared into the forest, all in different directions, they didn't know where. Because where do you live when you might not even exist?

21

The hedgehog was still lying in the darkness under his bed.

This is where I'm safest, he thought. Lonely and safe. It's also where it's easiest to be me.

He could sleep there for a very long time, sometimes even months, whereas in bed under his blanket he could only sleep at night-time and always woke up in the morning.

His prickles were lying flat on his back and creaking, as if they were groaning and disagreeing with something. They're not happy, he thought.

'I'm sorry,' he whispered. He knew that they preferred to stand up straight. They often wanted something different from what he wanted.

He tried to explain what he was doing there.

But they didn't say anything in reply.

'Talk to me!' he said. 'Talk to me!'

He wished they'd say something back. Like the horns on the giraffe's head, even if the giraffe was the only one who'd ever heard them say anything.

Maybe they only talk when I'm asleep, he thought. Are you comfortable? Yes, I'm fine. Could you move over a little? Sure, no problem, but then you have to move back a little. Is this far enough? Yes. He can snore, can't he? You're not kidding! I'm glad he's asleep. You can say that again. Shall we swap for a while: you on his back, me on his forehead? I wish we could! Shhh! Not so loud. Careful, he's waking up!

The hedgehog sighed.

If they could talk, he thought, they could also sing. Then they could form a choir. With the high voices at the front just above my eyes and the deep voices all the way at the back. If visitors came, they could sing a welcome song. 'Our hedgehog says you're welcome, come in and have some tea.' Swaying to and fro on my back in time to the music.

He would put a sign outside in the grass in front of his house:

PRESENTING THE BIG PRICKLE CHOIR.

ALL WELCOME.

UNPLEASANT VISITORS INCLUDED.

Then it wouldn't matter if someone was unpleasant. The prickle choir would make them pleasant, whether they wanted to be pleasant or not.

Hundreds of animals would come.

The giraffe would be flabbergasted. She'd be in a state of pure flabbergastation! She'd wish she had a hundred horns instead of just two.

What are two horns anyway… the hedgehog would say. A duo maybe, but no choir.

He tried to picture himself with only two prickles, one on his forehead and one on his back.

He shuddered and curled up a little tighter. Fortunately he had a hundred or even more. He could even give one or two away if someone really wanted one. And when winter came, he thought, the choir would sing a lullaby, very quietly, all winter long. His prickle choir.

Then he fell asleep.

22

The hedgehog had fallen asleep under his bed and was dreaming that he was reading a book. It was called *The Pros and Cons of Visitors.*

The first part was about the bad side of having visitors. The hedgehog read it and felt his heart pounding.

There were chapters about all the things that could go wrong before, during and after a visit: heated arguments, stale cake, salty tea, bitter accusations, malevolent glances in both directions, painful misunderstandings, uninvited guests, visitors who stay too long, chairs that fold when someone sits on them, visitors who sing songs they've made up themselves and ask everyone to sing along, and much more.

There seemed to be no end to the disadvantages of visitors. I don't want any visitors, he thought as he read.

Finally he came to the second part, 'The Advantages of Visitors'.

It consisted of a single short chapter that was made up of just one sentence: 'The advantages of visitors are not worth mentioning.'

Not worth mentioning, thought the hedgehog, not worth mentioning... He put the book aside and woke up. I'm not worth mentioning either, he thought, turned over onto his other side and went back to sleep.

A little later he had another dream.

The animals were dancing together and whispering in each other's ears:

'Will you come to visit me?'

'Yes, gladly, and will you come to visit me again after that?'

'Oh, I'd love to, and then you me again?'

'You bet! And then next time at my place...'

Everyone was really keen to visit everyone.

A little later he was walking through the forest and all the animals were racing past at top speed without saying hello.

'Why aren't you saying hello to me?' he called after them.

'We're out of breath. We're going to visit!'

'Who?'

'Each other.'

'And what about me?'

But they couldn't hear him any more.

He woke again with a start, out of breath himself.

He got out from under his bed, paced his room and looked out of the window. It was the middle of the night.

He crawled back under the bed and was soon asleep again.

For the third time that night he dreamt. He got hundreds of letters from all the animals.

'Are you finally going to come and visit me for once?'

'If only you knew how terribly much I'd love you to come visit…'

'Why don't you come now, right away?'

'You do realise I'll be at my wit's end if you don't come immediately.'

He went out of his door to visit everyone and when he reached the glade in the forest, all the animals were there.

'Ah, there you are!' they called. 'How lovely! Visiting me. And me!' They thronged around him, beamed at him, stuffed cake into his mouth and told him he'd come just in time. They couldn't have borne another second without him.

'Oh, Hedgehog, Hedgehog…' they called and sang.

And they said, 'You know what, you fly so gracefully too, Hedgehog.'

'But I can't fly!' he exclaimed.

'Of course you can – you shouldn't be so modest.'

They picked him up and threw him up in the air. 'See how well you fly!'

He fell down on the ground with a thud.

'Next time you'll manage it,' they said, patting him on the shoulder.

'Careful!' he cried. 'They're prickles!'

'Not at all,' they said and patted him on what he was sure were prickles with their hands and feet and wings and fins. Even the butterfly patted him with his wings.

His prickles were being pushed into his body. They patted him and patted him until only stubble was left. 'Look,' they said, 'the hedgehog's got stubble. Now he's the hubblehog!'

Then he woke up with a start, sat up, banged his head, didn't know where he was, remembered, sighed, lay down again, turned over onto his side, felt that he was covered with prickles, fell asleep and didn't have any more dreams that night.

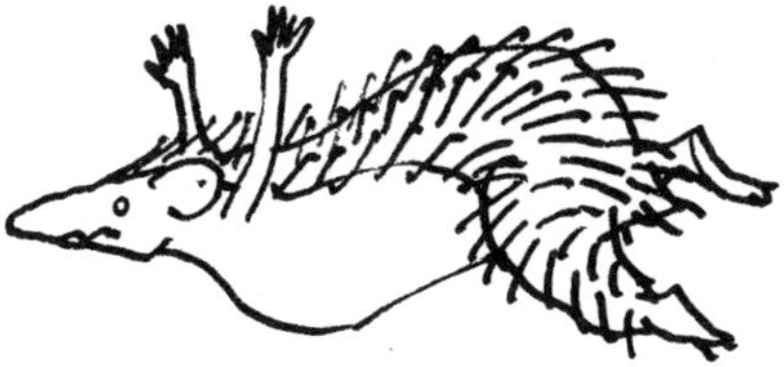

23

When he woke up, the day was dawning.

He looked at his room from under the bed.

My room, he thought. Nobody else's.

Sometimes his room was as big as the whole world. Maybe even bigger.

He looked at his door. It was on the edge of the world. If you went out through it, you'd fall into outer space and nobody could say where you'd end up.

He could see outer space through his window. It was green and mysterious. He shuddered.

His ceiling was the sky and his lamp, the sun. It only shone in the evening, but that didn't matter, not to him.

His table and chair were mountains and between his table and the window was the desert.

But where is the sea? He thought. And the river?

The river's here, he thought, between my bed and the table. I'll imagine that. That's allowed. Everything's allowed.

And the sea hasn't been discovered yet. I've never even heard of it.

He heard the ripples softly murmuring in the river and settled down in the grass on the bank. That's where the willow was too.

This is so lovely… he thought.

He forgot everything, including his loneliness and the autumn and the letter in his cupboard he hadn't sent yet.

Through his window he saw a fluttering speck.

The butterfly, he thought. 'Hello, Butterfly!' he called.

It *was* the butterfly. 'Hello, Hedgehog!' the butterfly called back.

'Careful,' the hedgehog shouted. 'You're flying around in outer space out there and if you land in it…'

'What?'

'I don't know.'

I really don't know, he thought. I'll have to think of something. But not now.

He closed his eyes and leant back in the grass on the bank of the river that flowed between his bed and the table and glittered in the light of the sun, high in the sky.

Nobody disturbed him or dropped by unexpectedly.

24

It's all so complicated, he thought a little later, when his room had gone back to being his room again.

He crawled out from under the bed and decided to go for a walk to think about the letter he still hadn't sent. Maybe that will help me decide, he thought.

He went outside and walked past the undergrowth next to his house on his way to the glade in the forest, where he bumped into the ant.

Shall I invite her right away? thought the hedgehog. Then I won't need to send the letter, and afterwards I might not need to have anyone else come to visit.

But he only said, 'Hello, Ant.'

The ant seemed lost in thought, looked up and said, 'Hello, Hedgehog.'

They stood there for a moment. The hedgehog hoped that the ant would say something, but she didn't. I'll just have to say something, thought the hedgehog. But what?

And without meaning to say it out loud, he said, 'It's all so complicated!'

The ant nodded. 'You're not wrong there, Hedgehog,' she said. 'Everything is complicated.'

'Everything?' the hedgehog asked. He thought about deciding whether to invite the animals. That was complicated. But there were lots of things that weren't complicated too. The rain, the wind, the rustling of the trees... They weren't complicated, were they?

'Yes,' the ant said. 'Name something that isn't complicated, according to you.'

The hedgehog thought for a moment, then said, 'The sky.'

'The sky!' the ant cried. 'That's the most complicated thing there is!' and she jumped up, did a somersault, fell on her back, got up again, brushed the dust off her shoulders and said, 'Something else.'

The hedgehog said the ground, the forest, the clouds, but the ant insisted that they were all very complicated, each more complicated than the rest.

Finally the hedgehog decided to name something that he did find complicated.

'You,' he said.

The ant stood still, thought for a moment, nodded, then said, 'I'm simple, Hedgehog. Very simple. I'm actually the simplest thing in the whole world. As far as that goes, I'm a miracle.'

The hedgehog stared at her with big eyes.

Then the ant leapt up and said, 'But that's very complicated. Simple is complicated. The simpler, the more complicated. I'm the simplest and most complicated thing in the whole world.'

She stood still again and cleared her throat.

The hedgehog didn't ask her anything else. He'd wanted to ask if visits were complicated, but he was scared the ant's answer would be more complicated than the question.

They said goodbye and the hedgehog walked on a little further, then headed home.

There, he went over to his mirror and looked at himself.

'Hello, Hedgehog,' he whispered. 'Are you here again? Have you come to visit, perhaps? Yes. How nice of you. I never get any visitors. And I never go to visit anyone either! How funny. Yes.' He gave himself a friendly smile, pointed out a chair, asked if his guest would care for something to drink, put on some tea, sat down opposite him, conversed about their shared prickles and mutual loneliness, said goodbye after a while, saw him off, sighed with relief, pressed his nose against the mirror and squeezed his eyes shut.

25

After some time he turned over and thought about the hippo. He could already see him trotting up.

'Hedgehog,' he called. 'I've come to visit you! I got your invitation. Open the door.' He was carrying something large on his back and was out of breath.

The hedgehog opened the door and the hippo tried to come in. But the thing on his back was too big.

'What is that?' the hedgehog asked.

'A tub.'

'A tub?'

'Yes, a bathtub.'

The hippo put the tub down in front of the door. 'I think I'll knock down part of the wall,' he said.

'Must you?'

'Yes.'

The hippo took a run-up and rammed the front of the house at full speed. The wall collapsed.

He cleared a path through the rubble, dragged the table, chair and bed outside, and put the bath in the middle of the room.

'There you go, Hedgehog,' he said, 'a present.'

'But…'

'Now you can have a bath whenever you like. Shall I show you how?'

He climbed onto the windowsill and dived elegantly into the bath, which was full of water.

An enormous wave washed over the edge and splashed up against what was left of the wall.

'This is how you have a bath,' he said.

He jumped up and down in the tub. 'I can't recommend it highly enough, Hedgehog.'

The wet hedgehog sat on the floor in a corner of his room and didn't say a word, thinking about how peculiar it was to have visitors.

After a while, the hippo got back out of the tub. '*Voilà*,' he said. 'A bath. For you, Hedgehog.'

The hedgehog didn't say anything and the hippo felt that it had been a very useful visit. He said he wanted to visit everyone and give everyone a tub so they could have baths too.

'Or maybe we should just flood the forest. Yes, that's it! We'll turn it into one big tub. Then we can all dive into it at the same time from the tops of the trees. What a splash that would make…'

He stepped over the pieces of door and wall, left the hedgehog behind with the bath and disappeared in the direction of the river, making a noise that sounded like whistling.

I don't want a tub, thought the hedgehog, I don't want any baths. I want a front door I don't have to open if I don't want any visitors, and I want it to be so thick nobody can walk straight through it.

26

Thinking of his door brought the woodworm to mind. She loved doors.

He could already see her approaching, already hear her calling, ‘That door, close it!’

‘Hello, Woodworm,’ the hedgehog said, and closed the door.

‘Hello, Hedgehog,’ the woodworm said, and bored her way in.

‘Would you like some tea?’ the hedgehog asked.

‘Tea? Can I bore into it?’

‘Hm… maybe with your nose… the smell…’

‘Perish the thought.’

‘Have you come to visit?’

‘No, I’ve come to do some boring.’

After an hour the hedgehog was surrounded by splinters and mouldering wood. He no longer had a bed, a table, chairs, a cupboard, roof, walls, floor or door.

'What now?' the woodworm asked.

'I don't know,' the hedgehog sighed.

'I'd like to bore into that too,' said the woodworm, 'your not knowing.' And she also wanted to bore into the hedgehog's prickles. She was very curious about what that would be like. She loved challenges, she said.

'My prickles are challenges,' the hedgehog said. He raised his eyebrows. What am I saying now? he thought.

A little later there was nothing left of anything.

Animals walked past the spot where the hedgehog's house had been and said to each other, That was where the hedgehog lived. The hedgehog? Yes, the hedgehog. Where does he live now then? He's history now. They explained to each other what history was and how you became it. Through the woodworm, for instance. But the woodworm was still there and heard them and said that she wanted to bore into history and into the future too, so that before and later and all the time in between, all the days, hours, minutes and seconds would turn to dust you could blow away. And when there was no time left anywhere, she wanted to bore into space and the void...

No, thought the hedgehog, I hope the woodworm doesn't come.

He made a sign and wrote on it:

WOODWORM: PLEASE BORE SOMEWHERE ELSE

After nailing it to his door, he thought for a second then crossed out PLEASE and added an exclamation mark after SOMEWHERE ELSE, and only then did he feel safe in his house, alone with all his prickles.

Although… safe? He couldn't be sure about that.

27

He sat down at the table, leant on his elbows and began pondering again.

Or maybe the grasshopper will come? he thought. Maybe she'll knock on my door tomorrow and want to start a shop.

It was still early, the sun hadn't risen yet and someone knocked on the door.

'Hedgehog!' they called.

The hedgehog got out of bed and shuffled over to the door.

'Who is it?'

'Me,' the grasshopper said, 'the grasshopper.'

The hedgehog opened the door and the grasshopper stepped in.

'Hello, Grasshopper,' said the hedgehog. 'Did you get my letter?'

'I did,' said the grasshopper, who looked around attentively, nodded now and then, and slid the table against a wall.

'This will be the counter,' she said.

'Of what?'

'Our shop,' the grasshopper said. She pulled open the curtains. 'That's why I'm so early. So we can be open later when the first customer arrives.'

She turned around. 'This is the shop window,' she said. She took a shelf out of the hedgehog's cupboard and laid it on the windowsill. On the shelf she arranged the hedgehog's jar of grass honey, his comb, his slippers and his small pointed scissors. 'They're for sale.'

She thought for a moment and then said, 'You know what? They're *on* sale!'

She made little notes and hung them on the bed – 'as good as new' – and the chairs – 'extremely sittable'. And she put a big sign in front of the door:

EVERYTHING INSIDE FOR SALE

Very soon animals arrived, wanting to buy something.

By the end of the morning the room was completely empty, and the grasshopper also put the hedgehog's coat up for sale for what she called a song, and the blue hat the hedgehog wore in the winter when he had cold ears.

After the weasel had bought the hat and the hippo the coat, the grasshopper looked thoughtfully at the hedgehog's prickles.

'Shall we sell them too?' she asked. 'Two for the price of one? There's sure to be a lot of interest. Shall I pull out a few and put them in the shop window?'

'Weren't you just coming to visit?'

'Visits! We'll sell them too. Of course! There's always demand and we've just got a new supply in: autumn visits, in all shapes and colours. The latest fashions. Thank you, Hedgehog, for reminding me. We'll put them in the display right away. We've got something for everyone.'

The hedgehog didn't say another word.

28

The snail and the tortoise would still be on their way at least, the hedgehog thought, once the grasshopper had disappeared from his thoughts. I'm slow, but they're slower.

'Tortoise!' called the snail.

'Yes.'

'Stop for a moment.'

'Why?'

'I want to ask you something.'

'Ask away.'

'I can only ask if you're standing still.'

The tortoise stopped.

'You never stand still, do you?' said the snail.

'Yes, I do. I stand still really often.'

'When?'

'Now.'

'Now… that's not standing still.'

'What is it then?'

'Waiting until I ask you something. That's not real standing still.'

The tortoise didn't answer.

'You don't even know what it is to really stand still,' the snail said.

The tortoise looked at the ground and didn't say anything.

'Are we halfway yet?' the snail asked. 'That's what I wanted to ask.'

'No.'

'Halfway to halfway?'

'No.'

'What about half of that?'

'No.'

'What are we halfway to, then?' the snail said with his tentacles sticking straight up. 'We must be halfway to somewhere?'

The tortoise sighed and said, 'Shall we keep going?'

'Wait a moment.'

'What for this time?'

'I asked you something! And we agreed that if I ask you something, we both stand still, otherwise I can't ask and I'll never find out what I want to know and we'll be lost. Hopelessly lost, in my case. Thanks to you. Or do you disagree with that too?'

'But what did you ask?'

'If you could stand still for a moment.'

'And then I asked why.'

'And then I said, I want to ask you something.'

The tortoise didn't say anything.

'See,' said the snail, 'I'm right.'

The tortoise started walking again.

'Leave, then!' screamed the snail, going red in the face. 'Don't let me disturb you! Leave your friend fumbling in the dark. Do you know who you really are under that shell of yours?'

'No,' the tortoise said and turned around. She knew she was the tortoise, but in the eyes of the snail she was often someone else.

'Ha! Now you can stand still, can't you, now you want to know who you are.'

'The lightning bolt?' the tortoise asked. Because that was something the snail often compared her to.

'No.'

'The emergency case?'

'No.'

'The quick-quick?'

'Yes, that too, but I mean someone else.'

'Who?'

'As long as you're standing still, I won't say, because then you're not her.'

The tortoise started walking again.

'Now you are!' the snail shouted.

'Who?' the tortoise called without stopping.

Now I have to say something, thought the snail. He crept into his shell and whispered – so quietly the tortoise couldn't hear – something terrible.

The tortoise took a few more steps, looked back and saw that the snail had disappeared into his shell. She felt a strange feeling coming over her. Dejection, she thought. But that wasn't it. Resignation. That was it. Quiet resignation.

She lay under her shell and fell asleep.

Then the snail fell asleep too.

I don't think they'll ever come, thought the hedgehog.

29

But the camel, he thought, he'll come one day. All the way from the desert. Running for days on end. Just to visit me!

The hedgehog felt his heart pounding. All because of my letter, he thought, at least if I ever send it…

He pictured the camel. Still panting and thirsty.

The hedgehog made three buckets of tea for him. And quickly whipped up a couple of sandcakes.

The camel ate and drank.

Then he leant back and looked around with surprise.

'What's that?' he asked, pointing.

'A chair,' said the hedgehog.

'And that?'

'A bed.'

'And that?'

'A window.'

He pointed everything out and kept shaking his head. According to him, all these things were pointless.

'And that?'

He pointed at the prickles on the hedgehog's back.

'Prickles.'

'Are they yours?'

'Yes.'

'I've never seen anything quite as futile. Aren't you embarrassed to walk around with something like that on your back?'

'What about those two humps on yours?' asked the hedgehog, who wasn't enjoying the conversation.

'They're pointless too!' the camel exclaimed. 'I find them deeply embarrassing. If only you knew! Would you like them?'

'No,' said the hedgehog.

But the camel pulled the two humps off his back and put them on the hedgehog's, pinning them into place with his prickles and then pounding them down with a couple of blows of his fists so the hedgehog wouldn't lose them. 'There you go,' he said.

Relieved, he immediately left and ran back to the desert, where he would be all alone. How fabulous, he thought on the way, nothing on my back any more!

The hedgehog shuffled over to the window with the two humps wobbling side to side on his back.

Then he sat down and wrote a letter to the camel saying he'd like to come and visit him sometime in the desert, but the camel mustn't come to visit him. It wasn't convenient. It got dark early. He had prickle-ache. Everybody was already coming. It was raining. He didn't have a thing in the house. There was no room for anyone else. The weather was bleak.

He thought of even more excuses, wrote them all down, explained what rain and bleak were, then threw the letter through the window and up into the air and watched it fly off in the direction of the desert.

30

Maybe soon it will rain so much the whole world will end up underwater, he thought, even the desert. If that happens, the carp and the pike will be sure to accept my invitation.

His door flew open and an enormous flood of water swirled into his house.

'What's happening?' he cried as he climbed onto the table.

He saw the carp and the pike swimming around his table in delight and sticking their heads up out of the water every now and then.

'Hello, Hedgehog,' they said, waving their fins.

'Hello, Carp, hello, Pike,' said the hedgehog. The water was already up to the lowest prickles on his back. 'How long is this going to continue?'

'This is enough for us,' the pike said.

The water stopped rising and the carp and the pike relaxed in the splashing, murmuring waves that came half-way up to the ceiling.

They swam over to the cupboard and found all kinds of things they'd never tasted before on the lowest shelf, which was now underwater: willowherb tea, honey cake, cream…

'Can we have some of this, Hedgehog?' they asked.

'Of course,' said the hedgehog, who was now hanging from his lamp, as the water had kept rising after all.

The carp and the pike let out cries of astonishment every time they tasted something new.

'This is all so delicious…' the pike said.

'You can say that again, Pike,' said the carp, who seemed to be in a good mood.

When the water rose even higher, the hedgehog climbed up through the chimney onto his roof and from his roof into the linden tree as his house disappeared completely underwater below him.

The carp and the pike swam back out, looked up and said goodbye.

'We're going to visit the elephant now,' they called.

'Okay,' said the hedgehog.

He was already near the top of the linden.

After that, he'd have to swim for it, because what else was there for him to hold on to? The moon? The sun? But he didn't know if he could manage that.

31

The hedgehog took a deep breath and thought for a while about unforeseen circumstances and difficulties that could arise when you had visitors, all the while trying to hold firm and not give into doubts.

If I send that letter maybe even the crow will come to visit. Though it's very unlikely she'll come in. She never goes in anywhere.

'Why have you invited me?' the crow asked.

'Because I never get any visitors.'

'Why not?'

The hedgehog didn't answer.

The crow shuffled side to side mistrustfully and cawed, 'No reply, eh, no reply.'

'Would you like a cup of tea out there?' the hedgehog asked.

'By myself, eh? Everyone's drinking tea inside, but not me.'

'Not at all.'

'Yes at all!' The crow cawed those words at least ten times in a row. 'Yes at all! Yes at all!'

Then she cawed, 'You want something from me, eh?'

'Not at all.'

'Yes at all. You want to sell me on, neutralise me, hand me down...' Her cawing became more and more raucous. 'That's why you've got prickles, of course. To spike me. That's what it's called. Look, I've spiked the crow... And now I'm going to sell her on. Who'll make the first offer? Second-hand Crow? No need to be scared, she's neutralised. You'll walk through the forest and everyone will see me. Crow on a spike. Oh, how lovely. Did you spike her yourself? Yes, that's what my prickles are for. Oh, now we understand what they're for! But I wrote to her first. Really? Yes. What did you write? That I thought it would be lovely if she came to visit. And she fell for it? Yes. Poor Crow, she always falls for everything... Yes, she's so gullible... More than that. Shall I let you in on a secret? That's what she's for, to fall for things. Really? Yes. That's what we invented her for, isn't it? True. Look, speak of the devil, there she is, the crow who always falls for everything. That's her. I see it. Look, she's spiked. Oh, how lovely. And now? Now?

There's no now about it. She'll stay spiked forever. That's the whole idea.'

She spread her wings and took off. 'That's it, Hedgehog: the idea. That's everyone's idea. And that idea is me!' And cawing loudly, she flew out of sight.

32

The hedgehog shook his head. But the lobster, he thought, she'll be sure to come in.

His door crashed open.

'There,' said the lobster.

'Hello, Lobster,' the hedgehog said quietly. He backed up carefully and went closer to the window.

'Visiting,' the lobster said in a sharp voice. She scurried up to the hedgehog and pulled a prickle out of his head with her pincers.

'Ow,' said the hedgehog.

'Louder,' said the lobster, pulling out another.

'Ow,' said the hedgehog, a little louder.

'Louder still,' said the lobster. 'You know what pain is, don't you?'

She pulled two prickles out at once.

Tears welled up in the hedgehog's eyes and he moaned softly. 'Why are you doing that?'

'Why? Does there have to be a reason? I'm just doing it. Like just leaning back for no reason if I'm sitting on a chair. Or scratching my back.'

One by one she pulled out all of the hedgehog's prickles. The hedgehog whimpered, groaned, screamed and screeched, but the lobster kept saying that he had to whimper, groan or screech louder, that it was pathetic and definitely not like it actually hurt.

In the end the hedgehog was completely bare, without a single prickle on his whole body.

'Don't I get a cup of tea?' asked the lobster.

'Of course,' wept the hedgehog.

The lobster picked him up in her pincers and hurled him at the teapot. 'What a visit…' she sighed, 'so much trouble for a miserable cup of tea…'

'I'm sorry,' the hedgehog whispered, while trying to make tea as fast as he could.

The lobster drank the tea and also scoffed most of the cake that was in the cupboard. She threw the rest out of the window.

Then she pulled the door off its hinges, tucked it under one of her pincers and went outside.

'As a souvenir of this visit,' she said, indicating the door. 'I collect doors.'

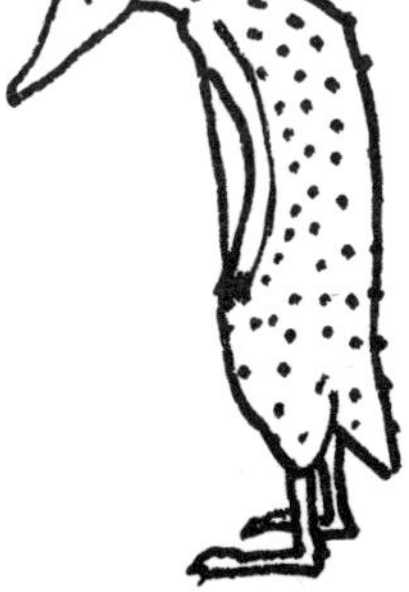

'Fine,' the hedgehog sobbed.

'Next time a little more pain, please.'

Then the lobster was gone, and the bare, cold hedgehog was standing in the empty doorframe the chilly autumn wind was blowing through.

He sat down at his window and resolved to build something impenetrable in the corner of his room, where the lobster would never be able to get at him if she came to visit. And nobody else either.

33

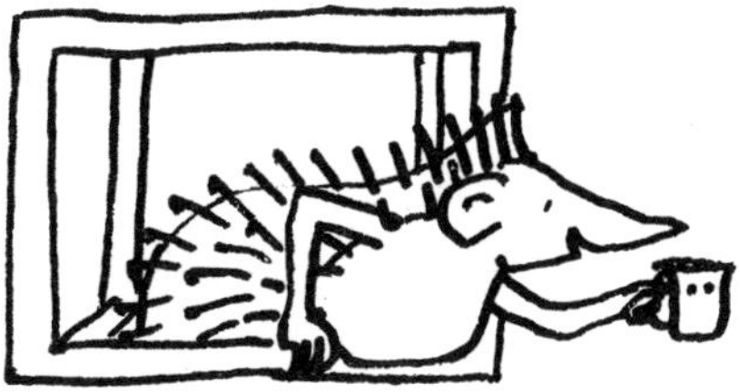

Including the wasp, he thought. He closed his eyes and saw the wasp sitting outside his window on a branch of the hawthorn tree, next to the linden.

The hedgehog opened the window wide.

'Hello, Wasp,' he said. 'Have you come to visit?'

'Yes,' said the wasp.

'You can come in.'

'I'd rather not,' the wasp said. 'If I get too close, I'll have to sting you with my sting.'

The hedgehog nodded. He knew. 'I've got prickles,' he said, 'but I never *have* to prick anyone.'

'We're different,' the wasp sighed.

The hedgehog put a cup of tea on the end of the branch the wasp was sitting on. He could just reach it if he leant as far out of his window as he could.

The wasp drank the tea – with lots of honey in it – and they started talking about stinging and being stung.

'It's so strange,' the wasp said, 'I *have* to sting, but otherwise I don't *have* to do anything: I don't have to sleep or fly or buzz… I like doing all those things, and I do them, but I don't have to. But I don't like stinging, and I have to. Do you have anything like that?'

The hedgehog thought about it.

'Doubt,' he said after a while. 'I don't want to doubt things, but I can't help myself. If I hope that someone comes to visit, I start to doubt my really hoping they'll come, and when I've eaten, I have doubts about whether or not to eat some more, and after I've woken up, I'm doubtful about whether I should get up. I doubt everything. I think that's strange.'

'Yes,' said the wasp. 'That is strange.'

They both fell silent, thinking that maybe you have to accept strangeness, whether you want to or not.

Then the wasp asked the hedgehog if he minded her coming inside for a moment anyway.

'Not at all,' the hedgehog said.

The wasp flew in through the window and sat on the windowsill next to the hedgehog.

'Would you like another cup?' the hedgehog asked.

'Yes… um…' the wasp said. 'I mean… I… oh, that terrible *having to* of mine…' and she turned towards the hedgehog.

The hedgehog ducked out of the way just in time and crawled under his table.

34

After the hedgehog had thought about a lot of animals he hoped wouldn't come to visit, he lay down on his bed.

He was tired, but it was too early to go to sleep.

I need to think of someone I'd love to have come to visit, he thought. But he couldn't.

He sighed. He was sure that everyone would be able to think of someone like that, everyone except him.

There's something wrong with me, he thought. But what?

He saw himself walking through the forest without prickles. It was winter. He was wearing a thick, black coat over his bare body. He shuffled through the mud and missed his prickles.

He'd thrown them away, into the river, and seen them float off towards the sea. Maybe the whale had found them there and put them on her back.

'I've got a fence. Look! A fence!' she shouted. The prickles were arranged in a circle around her fountain.

It started to snow. The hedgehog couldn't make any more progress. He was far from home, on the edge of the forest where nobody lived.

He shivered. What is wrong with me? he thought and cried, 'Help! Help! Who knows what's wrong with me?' But no answer came.

Suddenly summer began and it got very hot. He hardly had time to take his coat off. He was in the desert. His black coat trudged along behind him. The sun had a trunk and big ears. Time was gnawing on the back of his neck.

Then he fell asleep.

In the middle of the night he woke with a start.

'Who's there?' he called. He thought he'd heard something. But it was the wind banging on his door. He cautiously felt the back of his head. Prickles.

The top of his head. Prickles. His back. Prickles.

Prickles and visits and what's wrong with me – I don't care about those three at all, he thought. Not at all. Other things, I do. Then he fell asleep again.

35

When he woke up, it was still dark. He heard the floor creak. But I'm not dreaming, he thought. I'm sure of that.

He couldn't understand why the floor was creaking. If I was dreaming there'd be a reason for it, he thought. He listened, but he couldn't hear anything else.

Maybe it's the mole and the worm, he thought. They live underground. Maybe they'll come to visit if I invite them.

He could already hear them.

'Hedgehog! Hedgehog!' they called.

They knocked on the floor.

'Yes.'

'We're almost there! Is it dark?'

It was evening, but not completely dark yet.

'Kind of,' the hedgehog said.

'Close the curtains.'

The hedgehog closed the curtains.

'Can you still see your hand?'

The hedgehog held a hand in front of his eyes.

'More or less...' he said.

'More or less, more or less...' said the mole and the worm under the floor, 'that's no good to us.'

They made him hang his blanket up in front of the window, over the curtains, and block up all the chinks with the material from under his bed.

Then it was really dark.

The hedgehog heard a loud cracking noise followed immediately by two voices. 'Here we are.'

By the sound of it, they were now in his room.

'Hello, Hedgehog,' they said. 'So this is where you live.'

'Would you like some tea?' he asked.

'Yes, please. Black tea.'

The hedgehog made a pot of tea by feel and poured two cups.

'Delicious,' he heard them say. 'At least, fairly delicious.'

A little later he felt a pair of arms around him.

'What's happening?'

'We're dancing,' said one of the two. 'You and me. What a fun visit!'

The other one said, from near the cupboard, 'Have you got anything else to eat?'

'What have you had so far?' the hedgehog asked.

'Two cakes and a jar of honey.'

'No, that's all, I'm afraid.'

'Do we have to make do with that?'

'Yes.'

He heard smothered laughter and fell over. They're laughing at me, he thought. They mustn't think very much of it all.

'It's nice of you to have invited us, Hedgehog,' said one of the visitors.

'But the hospitality's a bit frugal,' said the other.

'If not to say mean.'

'Where we live under the ground, there's oodles of mud.'

'I'm sorry,' mumbled the hedgehog.

It wasn't until hours later that it was quiet. They've left, he thought.

He took the blanket down from in front of the window and opened the curtains.

The sun rose.

There was a hole in the middle of the floor that the mole and the worm had disappeared through. They'd presumably taken his black slippers with them, because he couldn't find them anywhere.

The hedgehog got up and looked outside. It was raining.

36

The rain kept getting heavier and the hedgehog found himself thinking of the badger. He didn't know why. I never think about the badger, he thought. Why now?

He saw the badger standing in front of his door. He seemed hesitant.

The hedgehog opened the window. 'Badger,' he said, 'have you come to visit? Because of my invitation?'

'Yes,' said the badger.

A little later they were sitting across from each other at the table.

The hedgehog poured the tea.

After having stirred his tea for a while, the badger said, 'I don't know what to talk about.'

'Me neither,' said the hedgehog.

'What could we talk about?' asked the badger.

'I don't know.'

'When somebody else comes to visit, will you know then? Or will that visitor know?'

'Nobody comes to visit.'

It was quiet for a while again.

'I'm worried,' the badger said, stirring his tea again, 'that we won't talk about anything.'

'Yes.'

The badger cleared his throat and said, 'But that would be terrible. Then my visit would be a failure.'

The hedgehog didn't answer.

The badger told him that he had a list of things to talk about at home, but he'd forgotten to bring it and couldn't remember what was on it.

'I think it's in a drawer,' he said. 'When I get home, I'll have a look. But then it will be too late.'

'Yes,' said the hedgehog.

The badger stopped stirring his tea and looked at the hedgehog. 'Or shall I come back tomorrow? With the list? There's so much on it, we could talk for hours.'

The hedgehog didn't say anything. He wasn't sure he wanted the badger to come back the next day.

'Don't you have a list like that?' the badger asked.

'No.'

'So how do you know what you want to talk about?'

'I don't.'

The badger sat up straight, slid his cup to one side and started telling the hedgehog things he could put on a list like that: summer, the sea…

'The sea…' the hedgehog said quietly. 'I've never been there.'

'Me neither,' said the badger. 'That's why it would be excellent on a list like that. And maybe it's on the list I left at home. And if it's not on it, I'll definitely add it.'

He pulled his cup closer again and went back to stirring his tea.

'It's such a shame I forgot to bring it…' he said. 'There are so many things on it! We could have talked to each other for days. I could also put forgetting on it, as something we could talk about, forgetting things…'

He shook his head and didn't say anything else.

They drank another cup of tea and when it got dark the badger went home.

'Too bad, Hedgehog,' he said as he was leaving.

'Yes,' said the hedgehog.

37

Then he thought of the beaver. What if he came to visit…? He doesn't say anything. He just builds a wall right away, right through the middle of the room.

The hedgehog knew that the beaver loved having walls between him and everyone else.

He squeezed his eyes shut and heard the hammering and sawing.

'Are you enjoying yourself?' he asked when the tea, which he had let run through under the wall, seemed to be finished, and the cake too, which he had tossed over it.

'I'm working,' the beaver said.

The hedgehog wasn't enjoying it himself, but he didn't say that. As long as my visitor is having a good time.

The beaver kept working on the wall all day.

'I'm splitting your house down the middle,' the hedgehog heard him shout somewhere high above him.

He was sitting in one half of his house, on the side of his

half bed, which the wall cut straight through. The beaver was in the other half, up near the roof, hard at work.

Towards evening he couldn't hear the beaver any more.

Is my loneliness split now too? he wondered. Into two half lonelinesses?

It was a strange idea and he wished it hadn't occurred to him.

He was sitting at the left side of his window, looking out at the undergrowth and watching the clouds scud across the sky. They could suddenly grow bigger and cover the whole sky or just as suddenly break up again and vanish without trace.

What if I suddenly disappeared like that, he thought, and somebody came to visit… Isn't he home? Apparently not. Let's have a look: here's that letter of his. Yes, it really does say it, 'I hereby invite you…' If I invite someone, I make sure I'm home! And more animals are coming. They're all waving my letter. Isn't the hedgehog home? No. But he invited us? Yes! Some of them shout that they'd always suspected me of being like that… Disappearing just when somebody comes to visit! That's him all over. And then animals arrive who shout that I don't even exist. No? No, he's a figment of your imagination and figments don't exist!

He couldn't hear the beaver at work any more and there wasn't a wall or anything that resembled one any more either.

I do exist, he thought, sitting on the side of his bed wrapped in his blanket. Do you know what doesn't exist? Later. Later doesn't exist. Only now exists. And now I'm going to open my cupboard and eat my last pot of nettle honey, on the top shelf right at the back, which has existed for years under a thick layer of dust and whose contents are now going to vanish without trace.

And he went to his cupboard, grabbed the jar of nettle honey, and ate up every last bit of it.

38

After that he went outside.

It was autumn, the wind was blasting through the bare branches of the trees and the rain was pelting down on his back.

He shivered but didn't want to go straight back in because then he would get out the letter again and go back to questioning whether or not he should send it.

He forgot the beaver and thought about his prickles. How different everything would be if I didn't have them...

He squeezed his eyes shut and tried to imagine what it would be like to walk through the forest. Without prickles, but with horns, two horns on his forehead, and not a nose but a trunk, and wings, two wings on the side and a kind of tail wing as well, to change direction.

By trying really hard, he managed to imagine all of that at once. And what if I chirped too and was cheerful...

He pictured himself one morning, very early, striding through the forest with long, light-footed steps, flying over something now and then and looking around cheerfully, and he heard himself chirping and even singing, the way the thrush sang. And if it was my birthday, he thought, and I'd been given a house as a present, high up in the oak with a view of the sea, and I'd invited the porcupine to come to visit – and nobody else – and the porcupine asked me if I wanted to dance, and I said, 'Sure, if you like…'

He squeezed his eyes shut even harder and saw himself dancing with the porcupine, without prickles and with two horns and a trunk and wings he was using to float in the air around the porcupine, who still had all his quills and looked stunning.

Then his face clouded over. Of course, the porcupine stops suddenly and asks, 'Who am I actually dancing with? That's something I'd like to know!' Then I'll have to tell him that I'm the hedgehog and he won't believe me, and he'll call me a fraud. 'Where are your prickles?' he'll say, while giving me a searching look. He might even find me dangerous.

I'm not dangerous, he thought.

But maybe he won't say that. Maybe he'll say, 'I know that, Hedgehog. I know who you are. You're the most beautiful and most exceptional animal in the whole world.' And he'll give me a big hug and on we'll dance.

He went back inside. The wind buffeted his walls and squalls of rain lashed his window. That's how far I should think, he thought. Until he says that and we're dancing. No further. He wished that he could draw a line in his thoughts so that he would stop thinking at that point, but he knew that he always kept thinking and in the end he was always the hedgehog and had prickles and nobody would ever come to visit him, and that absolutely nobody would want to dance with him, not even the porcupine, and that it was autumn and might stay autumn forever.

39

But then he gave himself a good shake that made all his prickles rattle side to side, and thought of the nightingale. Maybe the nightingale would come to visit him!

It was late evening in spring, twilight.

The nightingale flew in through the open window and perched on the edge of the table.

'Hello, Nightingale,' said the hedgehog.

'Hello, Hedgehog,' said the nightingale.

They drank some tea and the hedgehog asked casually if the nightingale would maybe like to sing something.

'Okay,' said the nightingale.

He opened his beak and began a wistful song. It wasn't long before the hedgehog felt tears running down his cheeks.

He found it strange. I'm not in pain, he thought. And I'm not sad either, am I? But the tears kept flowing.

When the nightingale had finished singing, the hedgehog

crawled under the table, rubbed his face dry and reappeared. He hoped the nightingale hadn't noticed the tears.

They drank another cup of tea and said goodbye. The nightingale flew off into the night.

The hedgehog sat at his table alone in the dark for a long time. That was so beautiful… he thought.

He wished tears could flow down his cheeks again, now that the nightingale wasn't here any more. But that didn't happen.

He stood up, wrote something on a sheet of paper and hung it up next to his mirror:

I DON'T KNOW ANYTHING, NOTHING AT ALL

He didn't know why he'd written it and he had no idea why he'd hung it up because, if there was one thing he knew perfectly well, it was that he didn't know anything.

His brain was creaking. That's because of the nightingale, he thought.

Then he concentrated as hard as he could on thinking something else he also knew very well: that he wanted to go to sleep.

He got into bed, pulled up the blanket, heard the nightingale singing again and felt more tears running down his cheeks. Of happiness, he thought. These are tears of happiness.

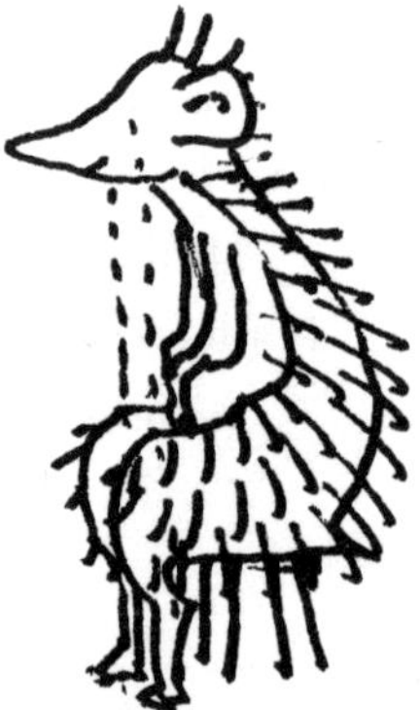

40

But he didn't fall asleep, and when the nightingale had finished singing in his imagination, he thought of the jellyfish. How strange, he thought. She's someone I never think of.

He saw the jellyfish before him, slowly floating in the waves. The sun was shining on the sea and every now and then the flying fish flew up out of the water in the distance.

The jellyfish had received the hedgehog's invitation and wanted very much to come and visit him. But how?

She looked around. I could swim to the beach, she thought. But then I'd need fins and a tail. And how do I get fins and a tail?

And if I had them and I swam to the beach, how would I get from there into the forest?

She pondered it more and more deeply. I'll need wings. But how do I get wings? And how will I know where to go in the forest?

How, how, how – that one word was always on her mind. When she woke up in the morning, in the breakers, she thought, how do I stay awake, and when she wanted to go to sleep at night, she thought, how do I get to sleep, and how do I dream that I'm the albatross or the dolphin, and in the daytime, when she was bobbing on the waves, she always thought the same thing, how can I be happy. Because she thought she wasn't.

The wind picked up and the jellyfish went under and came back up again.

And if I had wings and could fly and had flown to Hedgehog's house, she thought, how would I land?

She imagined four legs. But how would she get legs?

Then she'd need a coat, preferably deep blue. She loved blue, the colour of the sea in summer. And a blue hat and shoes, because otherwise she'd be sure to stand on something sharp when she tried to use those legs – which had never walked before.

And when she finally stepped into the hedgehog's house with fins, a tail, wings, four legs, four feet in shoes, a deep blue coat and a blue hat – without wondering any more how she would get all of those things – how was she supposed to act and what would she say if the hedgehog didn't recognise her? I'm the jellyfish, I've come to visit… Oh, so you're the jellyfish, the hedgehog might say. But how did you get here?

Yes, how… And then she'd have to sit down somewhere and the hedgehog would ask if she would like a cup of tea and how she took it. And how is she supposed to take her tea?

She shook her head and thought, no, I'll give that visit a miss. But how could she let the hedgehog know she wasn't coming? And she went under and came back up and went under again.

41

‘What do we actually have to do at the hedgehog’s?’ the snail asked as they trudged on.

‘I don’t know,’ the tortoise said.

‘I dunno, I dunno… You never know anything, do you?’ the snail said, stopping again. ‘You go to visit and you don’t even know what you’re going to do when you get there. What on earth! Do you know who you are really?’

‘No,’ the tortoise said.

‘The ignoramus. And if you had stripes, you’d be the striped ignoramus.’

‘I don’t have stripes,’ the tortoise said.

‘You don’t have anything.’

The tortoise looked at the ground. ‘We might have to dance,’ she said.

‘Dance!’ the snail yelled, his tentacles turning crimson. ‘Who with? The whale, I suppose…’

‘No,’ the snail said, ‘with each other.’

It was quiet for a moment. The snail was thinking. 'You and those sudden ideas of yours…' he mumbled.

But a little later they tried to dance with each other, very cautiously and very slowly, so they wouldn't arrive at the hedgehog's unprepared.

They bumped into each other, stumbled over each other, said 'ouch' a few times and decided in the end to just stand still.

'It's no good,' the tortoise said.

'See!' the snail said, and for a moment it looked like he was about to burst into tears. But he got a grip on himself.

'If the hedgehog suggests dancing, we'll tell him we'd rather just stand still,' the tortoise said.

'Standing still is a dance too,' said the snail. 'We can say that. It's called the standstill.'

They stood still for a while, then let go of each other again. The tortoise carried on. The snail stayed where he was. 'We can imagine we're visiting him here,' he said, pointing out a few sharp blades of grass on the side of the path that looked like prickles. 'That's the hedgehog. Hello, Hedgehog. Here we are. This is the tortoise. You know me. I'm the snail. We've come to dance. The slow standstill.'

'Come on,' the tortoise said.

'You're never any fun!' cried the snail. 'We just got here!'

42

The hedgehog was in bed. He closed his eyes and saw more and more animals who wanted to come and visit.

It was the start of the evening and they emerged from between the trees in the forest. But they kept their distance.

'Hedgehog!' they shouted. 'You invited us. But we're scared of you!'

The hedgehog was standing in front of his door. His house was decorated with streamers and paper lanterns, and there were cakes everywhere. He had been expecting them.

'There's no need to be scared,' he called back. 'There's nothing to be afraid of.'

'But we *are* scared. All those prickles…'

They didn't come any closer.

Then he attached the paper lanterns in his room one by one to the end of his prickles and went back outside. Hundreds of lanterns were swinging to and fro and lighting the trees and bushes around him.

'Are you still afraid of me now?' he called.

Step by step the animals came closer.

But when the first animal was close by, a lantern caught fire, and a little later they were all burning. The hedgehog screamed at the top of his voice and raced back inside like a burning torch.

It was night. Rain clattered on the roof and he woke with a start.

I was dreaming, he thought. He sat on the edge of his bed. Why can't I sleep without dreaming?

I'd be scared of me too, he thought. Those prickles… they're such weird, frightening things!

He crawled under his blanket and still didn't know whether or not to send the letter.

I'm weird, frightening, lonely and insecure, he thought. I have prickles, and I want someone to come and visit and at the same time I don't want anybody to come and visit.

What a strange animal!

Then he fell asleep.

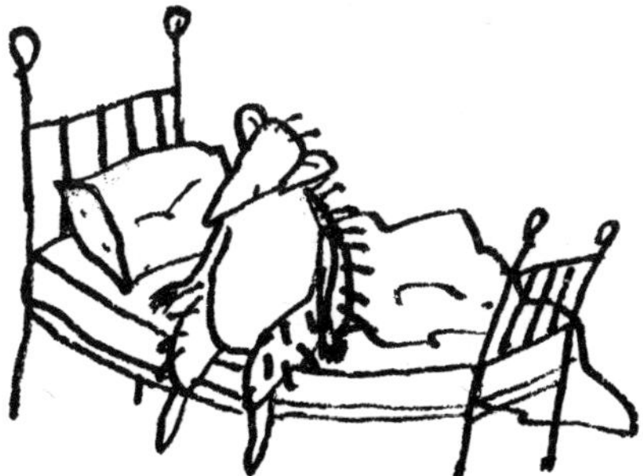

43

The May bug, the hedgehog thought the moment he woke up the next morning, he'll be sure to come!

He saw him buzzing towards him. 'Hedgehog, nice!' he called out from the distance.

'Hello, May,' the hedgehog said, once he had landed in front of him.

They went into the room. The May bug was beaming. He looked around.

'It's so nice here, Hedgehog,' he said.

'Do you think?'

'I think it's nice everywhere, but this is the nicest.' He sat down. 'I can't remember ever having been anywhere quite as nice before.'

The hedgehog made some tea.

Meanwhile the May bug stood behind the hedgehog and told him about everyone he had visited. It had been nice everywhere, even if there were small differences in the niceness. Giving examples, he explained the ways in which some places had been nicer than others.

'But this is the very nicest of all,' he said finally. 'Let there be no mistake about that, Hedgehog!'

'No,' the hedgehog said. He nodded, put two cups on the table and poured the tea.

They drank their tea and the May bug said that despite how nice it had been at the start of his visit, it kept getting nicer.

'It's almost unbelievable,' he said. He jumped up, knocking the table over in the process so that the cups fell on the floor and smashed, and the hot tea splashed up over the hedgehog. 'I didn't know it could get as nice as it is here now!'

He slapped the hedgehog on the shoulder from sheer delight, shouted, 'Ow!' sat down again, looked at his hand, pulled out a prickle, swallowed and said that even though it hurt, and quite badly, it was a nice kind of pain.

The hedgehog had never heard of pain like that before.

The May bug said that everything could be nice, even sorrow and despair.

'You don't know how nice it is to be desperate sometimes!' he exclaimed, waving his bleeding hand.

The hedgehog nodded and wondered if loneliness could be nice too. But he didn't say it out loud.

The May bug stared pensively at the new cup the hedgehog had put down in front of him, then leant back and said,

'To be honest, I think, of all the animals in the whole world, there's not one as nice as you, Hedgehog.'

'Really?' the hedgehog said, looking at the May bug with big eyes.

'Absolutely!' the May bug exclaimed. 'Let's dance.'

He leapt up and tried to grab the hedgehog, but hedgehog crept under the table.

The May bug was disappointed. 'But,' he said, 'I've never been disappointed this nicely before.'

The hedgehog held his breath under the table and heard the May bug leaving and calling out that it was a nice autumn and that they were about to get some nice rain…

44

The hedgehog paced his room, constantly imagining new animals that would come to visit, animals he knew but also animals that couldn't possibly come to visit, that might have gone extinct long ago.

He spent hours walking back and forth and racking his brains to think of the most unusual kinds of animals.

He also imagined that the animals he knew all had prickles, prickles just like his.

Here they came. The elephant with prickles that stopped him from climbing trees, because he got caught on every branch. The bear with prickles that were dripping with honey from the cake he had just rolled in. The butterfly with velvet prickles. The carp and the pike who stuck their prickly heads up out of the water and looked at each other with surprise. The ant with prickles who knew how everything worked. The mole with prickles the worm was strumming. The owl with prickles that each wrote their own letters. The snail with a prickle-shell…

They all had prickles and they were all coming to visit him.

'Hedgehog! Hedgehog!' they called. Thousands of animals. The prickly swift flew down to land, the prickled mouse came running up, the prickly tit tapped on his window…

Then he imagined, as so often before, that he didn't have any prickles.

'Hedgehog! Hedgehog!' they called again.

He opened his door and stood in the doorway. Smooth and shining in the light of the rising sun. He was the only animal in the whole world without prickles.

They all gaped at him.

'That's impossible…' they mumbled.

Some of them fled in terror, others fell to their knees, covered their faces with their hands and whispered, 'Hedgehog, Hedgehog, what have you done…'

None came any closer.

'Have you come to visit?' the hedgehog asked.

'Not any more,' they shouted.

'I've got tea and lots of cake to go with it.'

He saw that some of the animals were hesitating and the brown prickly bear was even about to take a step towards him.

But they didn't come closer, they said they didn't know how to act towards him and felt small and powerless with all those weird prickles, and they all disappeared into the forest or the river or crept into holes in the ground.

He went back inside.

Carefully he felt his back. I do have prickles, he thought. He would have called out after them, 'I'm one of you! I've got prickles too!' But they wouldn't have heard him any more.

He sat down at his table. 'There's no need for anyone to be scared of me,' he said quietly to himself. And he wished that they would all believe it.

He laid his head on his arms and slept.

45

But it wasn't long before he woke again with a start.

How long have I been asleep? he thought. Maybe days. Maybe all winter. It's like I'm always asleep…

But when he looked outside, he saw leaves falling from the trees. It's still autumn, he thought.

He stood at his window and thought about Snail and Tortoise. If he'd sent his letter they'd still be on their way.

He squeezed his eyes shut and imagined Snail's complaining.

'Why did he even invite us?' he asked.

The tortoise didn't reply.

'Why didn't he invite himself? Then he could visit himself.'

'How?' the tortoise asked.

'How what?'

'How can he visit himself?'

'How would I know?' the snail said. 'You and your hows. How this, how that. I'm not going to visit him.'

'You are.'

'I am what?'

'We are going to go visit him. You too.'

'That's the limit.'

'It's the way it is.'

'The way it is, the way it is... You and your never-ending way it is... Why don't you just stand still?' The snail thought for a moment and then continued, 'Why don't you have a proper shell?'

'I've got a shell,' the tortoise said.

'A shell! Of course! She's got a shell! But not a proper shell. Not one you can disappear into and close off. Shall I let you in on a secret?'

'What?'

'Everyone's got a shell.'

'No, they don't.'

'Really? Who doesn't have a shell then?'

The tortoise thought for a moment and then said quietly, 'The elephant.'

'The elephant!' the snail cried. 'He's got an enormous shell! But not a proper shell.'

'No, not a proper shell,' said the tortoise, who wanted to get moving again.

'See!' the snail cried, looking around triumphantly. 'He doesn't have a proper shell. I was right.'

He slid forward a little and then stayed where he was.

The hedgehog, at his window, opened his eyes and thought, I should write them a letter.

Dear Snail and Tortoise,

If you get a letter from me with an invitation to come and visit, you don't have to come. I would never hold that against you.

I'll come to visit you some time. In due course. Not right away.

THE HEDGEHOG

He scratched the back of his head. He could already hear the snail grumbling, '…have to, have to… him and his have to…' Maybe the snail would get really angry and want to come, to be the first one there, and start running, with the tortoise behind him, and come storming into his house in no time at all.

He decided that, whatever else, he wouldn't send them a letter like that, closed his eyes again, and saw them before him: shuffling, standing still, grumbling and inseparable.

46

Then he thought of the bison, who could run faster than anyone else. He would be sure to come too.

He pictured him far away on the plain. A letter floated down in front of him.

A letter! The bison had never had a letter before. It was an invitation to visit the hedgehog… The hedgehog!

The bison was touched. He immediately stopped grazing and started trotting in the direction of the forest.

Visiting the hedgehog! What did he actually look like? He had no idea. Maybe the hedgehog liked grazing and trotting and the plain too. But maybe he'd never been there.

The bison trotted as fast as he could. Maybe he would bring the hedgehog back to the plain with him so they could trot and graze there together. They were both so alone… Then they'd be happy together under the blue sky, the smell of grass in their nostrils, the plain under their feet and very,

very far away, the peaks of blue mountains that seemed to dance on the horizon, and always the sun high overhead...

The bison trotted for days on end. Maybe the hedgehog actually came from the plain but had forgotten. Maybe he too came from somewhere else and he'd forgotten that as well; maybe he'd once fallen out of the sky, and before that he'd trotted through the sky and grazed between the stars... That was why the night sky seemed so familiar...

He waded through the marsh, pushed through the brushwood and undergrowth, swam across the river and reached the first trees of the forest. He was almost there, at the hedgehog's! They would become friends; maybe the hedgehog could trot even faster than he could... But they would wait for each other if one of them needed to catch his breath and they would point out the juiciest grass to each other.

He started running faster and faster. He was already shouting, 'Hedgehog! Hedgehog!' He crossed the glade. There, that house, that must be the hedgehog's, he thought, but he couldn't slow down in time and flew at high speed, bellowing loudly in delight, right through the front door and into the hedgehog's house, and only came to a halt on the other side.

'Hedgehog! Here I am! The bison! Are you coming to the plain with me?' he called, looking back through the hole in the wall. He saw the hedgehog swinging to and fro on his lamp, which he had managed to grab just in time.

47

The secretary bird, the hedgehog then thought. He lives on the plain too. If he invited him, he would send a letter back but not come himself. He never comes himself. The ant once told him he doesn't even have a self.

The hedgehog squeezed his eyes shut and imagined a letter blowing in through his open window, floating around for a moment and then settling down and making itself comfortable on his table.

The hedgehog picked it up, held it against the light, and read it.

It was a cordial letter. The words were mild and melodious, letting him know how they were enjoying being read by him. They would gladly come to visit and hoped they would be welcome.

The hedgehog read each word slowly and carefully and sometimes three or four times.

When he had finished the letter, he thought, Do I need

to offer them something? But how do you offer something to words? What do they like? Not tea or cake.

He scratched between the prickles on the back of his head. Attention, he thought. That's what they like.

He gave them all the attention he could muster and read them again and they grew more and more cheerful and even more beautiful.

In the end they grabbed hold of him, pulled him up out of his chair, danced him round the room, hung off his neck, tickled him between his prickles and gently touched his lips with their Os and Us.

Supreme words, every last one carefully chosen. It was the most divine visit the hedgehog had ever had.

'Write back to us…' they whispered. 'Please…'

Then they disappeared, leaving only a blank sheet of white paper on the table.

The hedgehog opened his eyes. I have to write to him, he thought.

He pulled the piece of paper closer and wrote:

Dear Secretary Bird,

I hereby invite you to write me a letter in the near future, but one with words with lots of vowels in them and also unusual words I don't know yet and have to read over and over again until I understand them.

But I doubt you will write a letter like that to me because otherwise

Suddenly he didn't know what else he wanted to write and put down his pen.

He closed his eyes again.

Again a letter blew in through the open window.

From the secretary bird! he thought.

He quickly opened it and read:

Dear Hedgehog,

Otherwise what?

That was all it said.

The hedgehog rested his head on the letter on the table and thought, Maybe that's the unknown, something even the ant doesn't know about.

48

He sat up again, shook his head and decided to think about all the animals that could really come if he invited them.

He pictured the vervet, who lived on the other side of the world and had never been in the forest.

'Are you the hedgehog?' he asked.

'Yes,' said the hedgehog.

'I got your invitation. Here I am. I've never visited anyone before. What do I do?'

'Come in,' the hedgehog said.

'Do I have to?'

The hedgehog nodded and the vervet came in.

'Sit down,' said the hedgehog.

'Do I have to do that too?' The vervet looked around doubtfully.

The hedgehog nodded again and pointed to a chair.

'Do I have to sit on that?'

'You can sit on the floor if you'd rather.'

The vervet sat on the floor.

'And now?' he asked.

'Would you like a cup of tea?'

'Do I have to drink tea too?'

'No,' the hedgehog said, 'you don't have to.'

'What do you have to do if you're visiting?'

'Well, nothing really.'

'What are visits for then?' the vervet asked.

The hedgehog found that a very difficult question.

'I don't know,' he said.

'Are they not for anything, perhaps?'

The hedgehog thought for a moment and then said, 'Maybe we will have a nice time.'

'Aren't we already having a nice time?'

The hedgehog didn't say anything.

'Don't you know?' the vervet asked.

The hedgehog still didn't say anything and for a long time they sat together in silence.

The vervet was still waiting for an answer to his last question. When that answer didn't come, he asked, 'Is the visit almost over?'

'Yes.'

'Now?'

'Yes, now.'

The vervet got up and went outside. After a few steps he turned back and said, 'From now on I'm not available. Not for written invitations or any other kind either.'

'Fine,' the hedgehog said. 'Goodbye, Vervet.'

But the vervet had already disappeared into the bushes and didn't hear him.

49

Or, he thought, would the emperor pheasant stroll in one morning unannounced, straighten his feathers, cast a cool glance at his surroundings, stand at an angle to the window so the sunlight caught the tops of his wings, and observe him precisely? Subjecting him to inspection, as the emperor pheasant called it.

If he knew the emperor pheasant was coming, he would thoroughly wash his house and then himself, prickle by prickle, scrubbing and buffing.

Everything would shine. Animals that happened to be passing would be dazzled by the reflection of the sun on his window and quickly walk on.

That was how he would prepare for the emperor pheasant. But it wouldn't help.

The emperor pheasant would shake his head pityingly. 'Poor Hedgehog,' he would say. Yes, those would be his words, and with a simple hop he would jump up onto a chair and crane his neck to look on top of the cupboard.

'*Voilà*...' he would say, and ask the hedgehog to approach and then show him the speck of dust he had found on top of the cupboard.

'This is your undoing, Hedgehog,' he would say and hop back down off the chair.

And without another word, he would stride back outside with his beak in the air.

But the emperor pheasant would never come, thought the hedgehog, even if he begged him to. As far as he's concerned, I don't even exist.

He frowned and raised all his prickles.

But if he did come and found a speck of dust and strode back out with his nose in the air, I'd call after him, if I was brave enough, 'Emperor Pheasant!' and the emperor pheasant would stop, cast a weary glance over his violet shoulder and raise not only his nose but also his eyebrows.

And then the hedgehog would shout, 'You're undone yourself!' in his most strident voice.

It wouldn't make any sense, he realised that, but it would be satisfying.

Satisfying... he thought. What really satisfies me? He forgot about the emperor pheasant.

He looked around his old, dusty house, where the animals

would have to come for their visit if he sent the letter, and he couldn't see anything that really satisfied him.

Then he thought, My prickles, of course, they really satisfy me!

And he felt his chest swell with pride.

Let them come, he thought.

50

He was pacing his room when he suddenly heard a tremendous din in his thoughts, midway between sloshing and mooing.

That's the whale, he thought. She always turns up everywhere.

He saw her flying towards him, high above the oak.

The whale looked down.

'Is this where the hedgehog lives?' she called.

Animals raised their heads and called back, 'Hello, Whale. Have you been invited too? He lives there.' They pointed at his house.

'Have you already been to visit?' the whale asked.

'No, not yet,' the animals answered.

The whale flew down carefully and hovered in front of the hedgehog's door.

'Can I land here?' she called.

The hedgehog heard her and came out. Land... he thought. 'I'm not sure.'

'Shall I just stay here, then?'

'That's perfect.'

A little later the hedgehog was walking in and out with cups of tea, pieces of cake, salty cream and brackish water, because the whale was hungry and thirsty after her long journey.

Every now and then she sighed. 'Hovering is harder than swimming,' she said.

'Would you like to rest on something?' the hedgehog asked.

'Maybe…'

The hedgehog dragged out his table and the whale settled down on it. 'That's better,' she said.

The hedgehog was glad to help.

From the table the whale peered in through the window. 'Why don't you live at sea?' she asked.

'I don't know,' said the hedgehog, who had never even considered it.

'I wish everyone lived at sea,' the whale sighed, 'the giraffe, the cricket, the ant… that would be so nice… we could drop in on each other… give parties… a masked ball around my fountain…'

She stuck her tail up in the air. 'Oh, that's right. I'd almost forgotten. I've brought something for you.'

'For me?' the hedgehog asked with surprise.

'Yes.'

It was a tiny little fountain.

The whale attached it to the hedgehog's back, between his front prickles, and turned it on.

The water shot up and ran down over the hedgehog's back.

It was beautiful, but the hedgehog wasn't sure he was entirely pleased with it.

'How do you turn it off again?' he asked.

'It goes off by itself,' the whale said.

The forest around the hedgehog's house gradually flooded with water. The table with the whale on it began to float and a little later the whale swam in through the door.

'This is what I meant,' she said with a broad smile. 'Everyone at sea.'

Cries of 'What's happening?' were going up everywhere. Some of the animals saw what it was. The hedgehog has a fountain. Oh. Can't he turn it off? Apparently not. Oh.

Meanwhile the whale had gone back out through the door to swim back to the sea. 'I had a great time, Hedgehog!' she called back. 'Did you think it was a strange visit?'

'Yes,' the hedgehog shouted in reply.

'Will you come to see me for a strange visit too sometime? Then we'll both have a great time!'

The hedgehog could only just keep his head above water and no longer answered.

51

The hedgehog was sitting at his window and looking out, where mist was rising between the trees.

Maybe they'll expect something special from me, he thought. A dazzling reception. Tables covered with cakes. A hundred different kinds of tea. A choir. Maybe they'll be disappointed once they've come in and looked around, and say, 'What are we doing here? Call this a visit? This is pathetic,' then push me over, throw the grey moss cakes I've baked out of the window and be angry, angry and angry again.

But maybe I'll get angry then too, he thought. He felt his heart pounding. Maybe enormous rage will start to grow deep inside me and I'll shout, 'You didn't need to come!' Maybe all my prickles will stand on end.

'I can't help it,' I'll say, and tears will appear in my eyes, tears of rage, and I'll grab the elephant by his trunk and hurl him out through the open window, so far I hear him crying 'Whoa!' as he bangs into the oak. Then I'll call out,

'I'm sorry, Elephant, but I am so angry right now...' and then I'll hurl the giraffe away by her horns, the bear by his ears, the pike and the carp by their tails, the cricket by his feelers, the frog by his croak... Finally they'll all be up trees or floating downstream to the sea, whimpering, 'Hedgehog, Hedgehog... what have you done now...' 'My best,' I'll shout in reply, 'I've done my best...' and I'll sit down on the grass in front of my door sobbing in regret because I didn't want to get angry, I never want to get angry, and still I got angry.

Anger is an unnecessary evil, the ant once told him. The ant herself never got angry and always advised everyone against it. Although there were circumstances... she had added under her breath before walking on. What kind of circumstances? the hedgehog called after her, but the ant hadn't heard him.

Would they forgive me? he thought. They'll be sure to never come and visit again, even if I invite them a hundred times and write that I've decorated my house and there'll be a hundred cakes and two choirs.

He sighed.

No, that's all out of the question, he thought. Even if they're disappointed and throw me, my table, chairs and bed out of the window, I still won't get angry. But I'll regret inviting them, just as much as I'd regret nobody ever coming to visit.

He sat in a chair at his window thinking thoughts like these and he still didn't know whether he should send the letter. But he knew that when he finally knew something, it never took long before he didn't know it again.

The mist was turning into fog.

He opened the window a little.

There wasn't a sound to be heard.

It was autumn in the forest. Almost winter.

52

He cleared his throat, closed the window and thought some more about all the animals that could come to visit him.

The mouse. What would the mouse make of his invitation? She would study it thoroughly and compare it to all the other invitations she'd received over the years.

He could already see the mouse approaching in a black coat with a small red bow tie under her chin. She'd accepted the invitation.

'Hello, Hedgehog,' she called out before she'd even come close, 'is everything ready?'

'Hello, Mouse,' said the hedgehog when the mouse was standing before him. 'Ready for what?'

'For my introduction.'

'What are you introducing?'

'My visit to you in the context of visits in general. You've invited me, haven't you? Then I have to introduce my visit, surely? I'll keep it short. I propose I'll limit myself to a concise summary of what I could say.'

The hedgehog didn't reply.

The mouse stepped inside and looked around. 'The table there,' she said, pointing.

The hedgehog slid his table to one side. 'And the chairs there.'

The hedgehog slid both chairs to the other side of the room.

'Sit down, sit down,' the mouse said, 'make yourself comfortable.'

The hedgehog sat down and the mouse climbed onto the table, her coat flapping around her.

'May I welcome all present...' she began.

The hedgehog looked around but he was the only one present.

Would the mouse like some tea? he wondered. But it didn't seem like the right moment to ask.

The mouse cleared her throat and gave an introduction to the various aspects of visiting, mentioning the fabulous bright sides and the dismal, sometimes fatal, drawbacks, the grave misconceptions surrounding it, the pitfalls, the high hopes and the constant flow of astonishments and new perspectives it generated. She clarified her argument with several poignant examples: animals who returned home from visiting someone distraught and have been completely downhearted ever since; others who behaved exceptionally impolitely; yet others who, for no reason at all, burst into sobs and rent their garments, revealing their bodily peculiarities; and many more.

After the introduction, those present were allowed to ask questions.

The hedgehog asked if the mouse would like a cup of tea.

'That is an interesting question you have put to me there and I shall answer it with pleasure,' the mouse said. 'Very much. Thank you. No other questions? Then we have reached the end of my introduction and with it the start of the visit proper. Thank you, thank you!'

She bowed in all four directions, said that it had been one of the most attentive audiences she had ever had, and explained that she, despite her many stirring and discerning introductions, had remained modest. Pretension was completely foreign to her, she added with a slight catch in her voice.

The tea was ready.

'You must be tired,' the hedgehog said.

'Ah…' said the mouse, 'tiredness… let me talk about that next time. There's so much to say about it…' and she waved one hand as if brushing away something in front of her face.

The hedgehog wanted to ask her all kinds of things, but the mouse pointed to her throat and whispered, 'I have to go easy on my voice.' The hedgehog nodded.

It was only hours later, when the hedgehog's cupboard was bare and the silence had become almost intolerable, that the mouse went home.

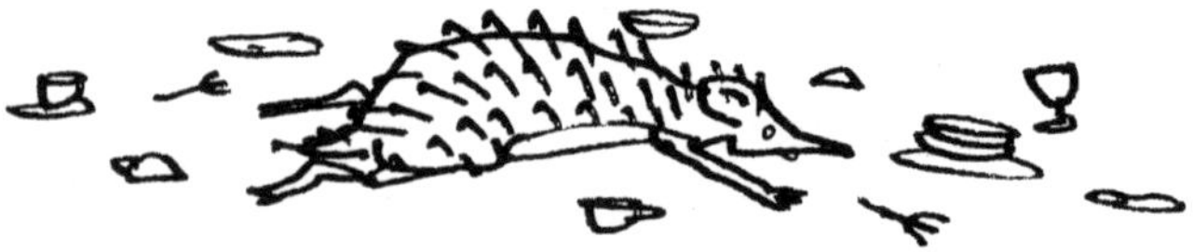

53

The owl, thought the hedgehog, once the mouse had faded from his thoughts – she'll be sure not to come. But she will write:

Dear Hedgehog,

Thank you for the invitation.

I won't be coming.

There are too many things in the way – in my way, I mean – for me to go and visit someone.

The darkness. I prefer to stay in it, unseen.

The tea. I don't like tea.

The topics of discussion. I never want to talk about the things other animals want to talk about.

The salutations on arrival and departure. I haven't mastered them.

What do you think, by the way, of existence? Do you think it's big or small? That's been preoccupying me lately.

Will you let me know? In writing, of course. Thank you for the invitation.

THE OWL

He would read the letter and think about the owl's question. Do you think existence is big or small?

Probably small, he thought. Maybe so small you can't see it. That's it! That's why he didn't see all those things: existence, life, happiness… They were all too small to see. Nobody saw them!

Then the hedgehog thought about something the ant had once talked to him about: death.

That was something small too, maybe the very smallest and most insignificant of all that existed.

If you had very sharp eyes like the owl's, maybe there was a small chance that, if you tried as hard as you could, you might be able to see life and happiness, but you still wouldn't see death. That was why everyone thought it didn't exist. It did exist though, presumably. That's what the ant said.

Presumably… the hedgehog had thought then. That was something like for all intents and purposes. It existed for all intents and purposes.

He'd shuddered, even though the ant had only shrugged and said that she always shrugged her shoulders when it came to death. You didn't have to think about it. It wasn't necessary at all. Then she'd cleared her throat and walked on.

The owl wouldn't come to visit, thought the hedgehog, and he decided not to think about existence and to definitely not think about death. He wondered if that would work.

54

If I'd invited everyone, he then thought, and everyone had come and gone back home, or had let me know that they never visited anyone or couldn't make it, the snail and the tortoise would still be on their way.

He pictured them again: the tortoise looking back, the snail standing still.

The tortoise sighed and asked, 'Would you like to sit on my shell?'

'On your shell?' the snail cried, his eyes growing big.

'Then we'll go faster,' the tortoise said.

'And then what? Then we'll end up losing control on a corner so that I'll fall off and crash full speed into a tree, with me breaking my shell and you telling me how sorry you are for going too fast again and that you really didn't mean it. But you do mean it, Tortoise, you always mean it!'

'I never mean to lose control on a corner.'

'What difference does that make if my shell's shattered and you're offering to put it back together again with that speedy voice of yours?'

'Wouldn't you want that?'

'Insult to injury! As if I'd want to live in a ruin… With a sign out the front: MORE HASTE. That's what the ruin will be called. And a sign next to it saying you're to blame.'

The tortoise didn't say anything.

'I'll go at my own pace,' the snail said.

'You mean you'll stand still.'

'That's part of my own pace.'

They stood still for a while.

'We'll never get there this way,' the tortoise said.

'If I close my eyes I'm already there,' said the snail.

The tortoise thought for a moment.

'Do you see the hedgehog?' she asked.

'Yes.'

'What's he look like?'

'Grey. With those big ears and a trunk.'

'That's the elephant.'

'The elephant, the elephant… you and your elephant… Do *you* know what the hedgehog looks like?'

The tortoise thought again and then said, 'No. I don't. But we need to speed up a little.'

'Speed up! Of course! It gets better and better! Shoot off the path, you mean, speed into a tree… Why don't you fly, then you'll be there in no time.'

'I don't have any wings.'

'No, heaven forbid… You with wings, what a spectacle!'

'But I *don't* have any wings… Or shall we just go back?'

'Go back… You and your going back… Why don't you ever stop to think before you open your mouth?' the snail said. He gave a little cough. 'If you did, you'd never say anything.'

The tortoise fell silent and resolved to never ask the snail anything ever again. She heard a vague but slowly growing hum from the direction of the hedgehog's house. Now they're cutting the cake. Now they're tucking into it, she thought. Now the visit is reaching its climax.

She took a deep breath and looked back at the snail.

55

Maybe the tortoise will come by herself, thought the hedgehog.

He could already hear her knocking on the door.

'Who is it?' he asked.

'It's me. The tortoise.'

'Come in.'

'We got your invitation, Hedgehog,' the tortoise said, 'the snail and I.'

'Hasn't he come with you?'

The tortoise shook her head. 'No,' she said, 'it was all too fast for him.'

'What?'

But the tortoise was shaking her head again. 'He's my friend,' she said.

'Where is he now?'

'Somewhere,' the tortoise said. 'He's waiting for me. He sends his love, I'm sure of that. He is always so attentive.'

The hedgehog put on some tea.

For a long time they sat silently together and drank their tea.

The tortoise peered at her cup with a gloomy expression. 'I'm too fast for him,' she said. 'Much too fast. He is a miracle of slowness, Hedgehog. And he keeps getting slower!'

She fell silent again. But a little later she cleared her throat and told the hedgehog that the snail had recently compared her to a lightning bolt.

'Do you think that too?' she asked. 'Me bursting in here like this… He's probably right.' She coughed. 'I'm bad weather, according to him. Stormy weather. That's what he calls me sometimes. A storm in a shell.' She looked at the hedgehog and swallowed. 'I wish that we were here visiting you together, Hedgehog. He would enjoy it so much…' she said. 'When we're together, we're the most beautiful weather in the whole wide world.' She took a deep breath. 'We're timeless.'

The hedgehog saw that there were tears in her eyes. They're real friends, he thought.

'Shall I give you something for him?' he asked. 'Something tasty, perhaps?'

But the tortoise shook her head. 'He's completely self-sufficient. He's always saying so.'

'Isn't there anything he wants?'

'A complete standstill,' the tortoise said. 'Everything standing still. Not just him, but me too, and everyone else and the whole world.'

They sighed deeply and both thought, That's impossible. The tortoise also thought that it was terrible that it was impossible, and the hedgehog thought it was a pity, but maybe not.

Then the tortoise left again. 'I'm going back to him,' she said, turning slowly. 'You'll wait for me, won't you?' the hedgehog heard her whispering. 'I'm coming. I'm your friend, aren't I? I can't go any slower. I'm sorry…'

The hedgehog stood in his doorway and watched the tortoise shuffle off cautiously into the undergrowth.

Then he went back inside, feeling lonely.

56

Maybe I need to write a different kind of letter, he thought:

Dear animals,

Maybe one of you is planning on visiting me sometime soon.

Because they think it will be nice.

Or because they're curious about nobody ever visiting me and want to tell everyone what it was like afterwards.

Do not put that plan into practice.

I am not nice.

I have prickles.

I never know what to talk about.

I can't dance and I can't sing either.

Even I don't like the tea I make and the cake in my cupboard is so stale it's turned grey.

I'm nothing special.

I am nothing.

So don't come.

HEDGEHOG

Or would that just make them come? he wondered. So they can tell me that I am very nice and that they think my prickles are beautiful. And that they already know what they want to talk about and so they can wrap their arms around me and dance with me and then fall over with blood everywhere, and say how well I dance, wonderfully, in fact, and I'm undoubtedly a good singer too and make delicious tea and that stale cake is their favourite and that I am something, they don't know what yet, but they'll find out!

He saw them stand up and wrap their arms around him again, softly groaning, and he heard them say that he was their very best friend, because they wouldn't go through something like this for their second-best friend. Never in a thousand years.

He went over to his window and looked out. The mist had cleared. It was raining.

Maybe I only want visitors so I can find out that I don't want visitors, he thought.

He opened the window and stuck out his head. The rain fell on the back of his neck and the drops zigzagged down between his prickles.

He stood there like that for a long time.

57

It was night, cold. The hedgehog was in bed and curled up as tight as possible. But he still couldn't get warm.

He heard noise outside. Rain, he thought. Or a storm. But it was neither rain nor storm.

The noise came closer. The hedgehog couldn't work out what it could be.

Then the door flew open and someone or something came in.

The hedgehog looked hard, but it was too dark to make it out.

'Who are you?' he asked fearfully.

'The monster,' said a voice near the ceiling. The monster seemed very big, bigger than the animals the hedgehog knew.

'What are you doing here?' he asked.

'Visiting,' the monster said. 'What else?'

Slowly it came closer. It smelt of old mud and dirty grass.

'Please, have a seat,' the hedgehog said, hoping the monster would sit down and not come any closer.

But the monster knocked the chair over.

'What are you doing?' the hedgehog asked.

'Visiting. You. You're the hedgehog, aren't you?'

'Yes.'

'Then this is where I'm supposed to be.'

The monster stamped on the chair, smashed the table and bashed the lamp off the ceiling with the top of its body. Maybe that's where its head is, thought the hedgehog, or maybe some other part of its body.

Then it picked up the cupboard and threw it through the window.

'Please leave,' the hedgehog asked.

'I'm visiting. I just got here.'

'I didn't invite you…'

'No?' It sounded menacing. 'Why not? Did you think, I'll invite everyone, but not the monster…? Or maybe you thought I didn't exist? Was that what you were secretly hoping?'

'I haven't invited anyone yet.'

'No? Nobody? Don't you want any visitors?'

The hedgehog crept as far away in his bed as he could.

'I do,' he said. 'I do want visitors and I hope not secretly. But I thought…'

The monster bent over him.

'Shall I tell you something, Hedgehog?' it said.

'No,' said the hedgehog.

'Then I won't,' the monster growled. It gnashed its teeth and grabbed hold of the hedgehog.

'Would you like some tea?' asked the hedgehog.

Then he was lifted up in the air. He heard a loud bang and then nothing.

58

The hedgehog woke up on the floor next to the bed. Who am I? he thought. I mean, who is anyone? I mean…

He looked at his room. Everything was where it always was. Obedient, he thought. Unmoved. Quiet.

He pushed himself up on his elbows, shuffled over to the cupboard, pulled the letter out of the drawer and tore it up.

No, he thought, I don't want anyone coming to visit. Now I know that for sure.

He grabbed his broom and swept the floor, looked in his cupboard to see what he had kept for the winter, made his bed and sat down again at the table.

He rested his head on his arms, closed his eyes and resolved to sit there like that for now. Not letting anything or anyone disturb him.

Then he heard a quiet knocking.

He sat up straight and opened his eyes. Someone was knocking on his door! But I haven't invited anyone, he thought.

There was another knock.

'Who is it?' he asked.

'Me,' a voice said. 'The squirrel. May I come in?'

'Why?'

'I don't know. No reason. I thought, maybe you'd like having someone come to visit.'

The hedgehog took a deep breath, looked left and right, stood up and opened the door.

The squirrel stepped in.

'Hello, Hedgehog,' he said.

'Hello, Squirrel,' said the hedgehog.

'I won't stay long,' said the squirrel.

They didn't say much more, but they did sit down opposite each other at the table.

The squirrel had brought a jar of beechnut honey with him. He thought the hedgehog might fancy a little.

'You're right there,' the hedgehog said, going over to his cupboard to get a jar of thistle honey he'd been saving for a special occasion. That special occasion had now come, he thought.

They drank tea, ate honey and nodded at each other every now and then.

In the course of the afternoon they hoped time would stand still or that the longhorn beetle might coincidentally choose that afternoon to turn seconds into hours and make the day last a whole year and that the tea and honey would never run out and they saw through the window that it was twilight and it started to snow and they hoped it would snow for a really long time, so that the front door wouldn't open any more and the squirrel might have to stay for the whole winter.

It would be fine by them. When they thought about it, they realised that everything was fine by them.

This was how one day at the start of winter the hedgehog had an unexpected visitor.

59

The hedgehog was asleep.

He was curled up in bed in a corner of his room, under the blanket. He wasn't dreaming.

Outside it was dark.

It was snowing and a gale was blowing and it was freezing cold, colder than ever before.

It was as if the wind was trying to break into the house and bring the snow and ice with it. As if they wanted to freeze his whole house and the hedgehog too, and bury them under a thick layer of snow and then blow it all away, up into the clouds racing over the forest, and maybe right out of the world.

But they couldn't.

In the middle of the night, he woke up. The storm was at its furious height. His house was creaking and squeaking and rattling. But he wasn't scared. If they really do come in, I'll raise my prickles, he thought. Then they'll back off.

His prickles were his rock and his bastion, even if he didn't know what a bastion was.

He crept a little deeper under the blanket and thought of all the animals he knew: in the forest, in the desert, in the middle of the ocean, on the riverbed, under the ground, high in the sky.

They all wrote him a letter in which they thanked him for not inviting them. They were all his friends and they would stay friends with him forever; they didn't need to come to visit.

Only the squirrel wrote something else: 'I had such a lovely time, Hedgehog,' and at the bottom, 'See you soon!'

The hedgehog closed his eyes and let out a deep sigh. See you soon… he thought. They were the most beautiful words he knew.

Then he fell asleep and slept all through the rest of the winter.

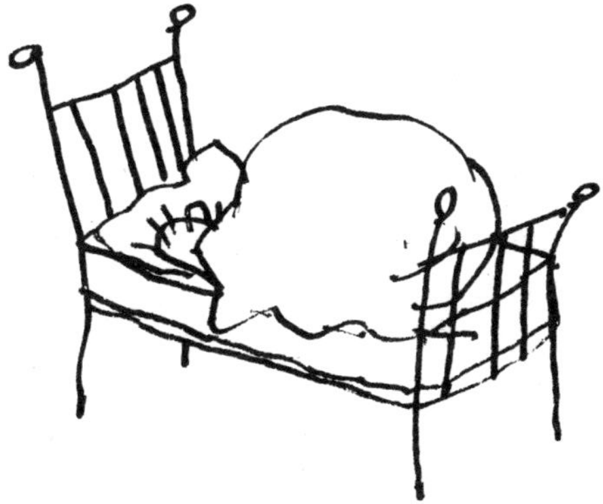

FORBIDDEN NOTEBOOK
ALBA DE CÉSPEDES

COLLECTED WORKS: A NOVEL
LYDIA SANDGREN

MY MEN
VICTORIA KIELLAND

AS RICH AS THE KING
ABIGAIL ASSOR

LAND OF SNOW AND ASHES
PETRA RAUTIAINEN

LUCKY BREAKS
YEVGENIA BELORUSETS

THE WOLF HUNT
AYELET GUNDAR-GOSHEN

MISS ICELAND
AUDUR AVA ÓLAFSDÓTTIR

MIRROR, SHOULDER, SIGNAL
DORTHE NORS

THE WONDERS
ELENA MEDEL

MS ICE SANDWICH
MIEKO KAWAKAMI

GROWN UPS
MARIE AUBERT

LEARNING TO TALK TO PLANTS
MARTA ORRIOLS

THE RABBIT BACK LITERATURE SOCIETY
PASI ILMARI JÄÄSKELÄINEN

BINOCULAR VISION

EDITH PEARLMAN

MY BROTHER

KARIN SMIRNOFF

ISLAND

SIRI RANVA HJELM JACOBSEN

ARTURO'S ISLAND

ELSA MORANTE

PYRE

PERUMAL MURUGAN

RED DOG

WILLEM ANKER

THE COLLECTED STORIES OF STEFAN ZWEIG

STEFAN ZWEIG

AN UNTOUCHED HOUSE

WILLEM FREDERIK HERMANS

WILL

JEROEN OLYSLAEGERS

MY CAT YUGOSLAVIA

PAJTIM STATOVCI

BEAUTY IS A WOUND

EKA KURNIAWAN

BONITA AVENUE

PETER BUWALDA

IN THE BEGINNING WAS THE SEA

TOMÁS GONZÁLEZ

TRAVELLER OF THE CENTURY

ANDRÉS NEUMAN